ATTIA HOSAIN

was born in Lucknow, UP, India, in 1913. She was educated
at La Martiniere and Isabella Thoburn College, Lucknow,
blending an English liberal education with that of a traditional Muslim household where she was taught Persian,
Urdu and Arabic. She was the first woman to graduate from
amongst the feudal, "Taluqdari" families into which she
was born.

Influenced, in the 1930s, by the nationalist movement
and the Progressive Writers' Group in India, she became a
journalist, broadcaster and writer of short stories.

In 1947, the year of Indian Independence, she came to
England with her husband and two children. Presenting
her own woman's programme on the BBC Eastern service,
amongst others, for many years, she also appeared on
television and the West End stage. In addition she lectured
on the confluence of Indian and Western culture, and
wrote *Phoenix Fled* (1953), a collection of short stories, and
Sunlight on a Broken Column (1961), a novel. She had
previously written stories which were published in maga-
zines in India, the United States and in Britain.

She now divides her time between London and India.

Attia Hosain

PHOENIX FLED

AND OTHER STORIES

WITH A NEW INTRODUCTION BY
ANITA DESAI

PENGUIN BOOKS — VIRAGO PRESS

PENGUIN BOOKS
Published by the Penguin Group
Viking Penguin, a division of Penguin Books USA Inc.,
40 West 23rd Street, New York, New York 10010, U.S.A.
Penguin Books Ltd, 27 Wrights Lane,
London W8 5TZ, England
Penguin Books Australia Ltd, Ringwood,
Victoria, Australia
Penguin Books Canada Ltd, 2801 John Street,
Markham, Ontario, Canada L3R 1B4
Penguin Books (N.Z.) Ltd, 182–190 Wairau Road,
Auckland 10, New Zealand

Penguin Books Ltd, Registered Offices:
Harmondsworth, Middlesex, England

First published in Great Britain by Chatto & Windus 1953
This edition first published in Great Britain
by Virago Press Limited 1988
Published in Penguin Books 1989

1   3   5   7   9   10   8   6   4   2

(CIP data available)
ISBN 0 14 016.192 9

Printed in the United States of America

CONTENTS

INTRODUCTION

In India, the past never disappears. It does not even become transformed into a ghost. Concrete, physical, palpable — it is present everywhere. Ruins, monuments, litter the streets, hold up the traffic, create strange islands in the modernity of the cities. No one fears or avoids them — goats and cows graze around them, the poor string up ropes and rags and turn them into dwellings, election campaigners and cinema distributors plaster them with pamphlets — and so they remain a part of the here and now, of today.

In other ways, too, the past clings. As sticky as glue, or syrup. Traditions. Customs. "Why do you paint a tika on your baby's forehead?" "Why do you fall at your father's feet and touch your forehead to the ground?" "Why does a woman fast on this particular day?" "Why bathe in the river during an eclipse?" "Why does the bridegroom arrive on a horse, bearing a sword?" It is the custom, the tradition. No further explanation is required than this — it has always been so, it must continue to be so.

If there is a break in that tradition, then — "What will happen?" Things too terrible to be named. The downfall of the family, of society, of religion, of the motherland, India herself.

So a woman will paint a tika on her baby's forehead, a young man touch an elder's feet, a marriage need to be approved not only by parents but an astrologer as well … and so life is lived according to its rules, rules prescribed by time, centuries of time.

Of course time moves in other directions as well — TV and radio sets invade homes, the sari is given up for jeans, the old astrologer laughed at and the priest avoided, the past scorned. But it remains. Like the colour of one's skin, and eyes, it remains. It does not leave.

Attia Hosain's novel and collection of short stories are monuments to that past: the history of north India, before Partition. A monument suggests a gravestone — grey, cold and immutable. Her books are not: they are delicate and tender, like new grass, and they stir with life and the play of sunlight and rain. To read them is as if one had parted a curtain, or opened a door, and strayed into the past.

That is their charm and significance. To read them is like wrapping oneself up in one's mother's wedding sari, lifting the family jewels out of a faded box and admiring their glitter, inhaling the musky perfume of old silks in a camphor chest. Almost forgotten colours and scents; one wonders if one can endure them in the light of what has come to pass. But guiltily, with a laugh, the reader can't but confess "Really? Is that how it was? It must have been —" Glamorous? Fascinating? Outrageous? Impossible?

What are the precise ingredients of that now difficult to visualise past? For Attia Hosain it was an undivided India in which Muslims and Hindus celebrated the same festivals and often worshipped at the same shrines.

Not only did he observe the rituals of his own religion, but in the month of Moharrum, he kept a "tazia" in a specially prepared shed. On the tenth day of the month, the elaborate man-high tomb made of bright-coloured paper and tinsel was carried to its burial in a procession. The Muslim servants recited dirges in memory of the martyred family of the Prophet, while he and his sons followed in barefooted, bareheaded respect. (Shiv Prasad, "White Leopard", *Phoenix Fled.*)

Society was not then in flux, it was static, and it was a feudal society. To know what feudalism meant, one has to read *Sunlight on a Broken Column* or *Phoenix Fled* and learn how it was made — how the land belonged to the wealthy *taluqdars*, how the peasants worked upon it, what was exacted from them and what was, in return, done to or for them. How women lived in a secluded part of the house, jealously protected by their menfolk, and what powers were theirs, or not. How deference had always to be shown to the ancestors, to the aristocracy, to the priests, who could choose either to exploit or harrass their dependents or, if they had any nobility of spirit, protect and nurture them. How the one unforgiveable sin was to rock this hierarchy, its stability. How no one could offend religion or the family or society by going against it and only those who lived according to its rules could survive.

Born in 1913, Attia Hosain came from a background and a family that equipped her with all the knowledge she needed to write these books. Her father was a *taluqdar* of Oudh, a state in north India that the British knew as the United Provinces, the home of nawabs who dazzled even the wealthy colonists by the splendour of their courts. She belongs to the clan of Kidwais that has produced many distinguished and prominent men of this century. Her father studied at Christ College, Cambridge, and the Middle Temple, and like other young men in his circle of contemporaries, became well known in the political and national movements of his time. A great friend of his was Motilal Nehru, the father of Jawaharlal Nehru. Attia Hosain's mother came from a family that had distinguished itself in another world — the intellectual one — and had been educated in the old Persian and Urdu tradition. When her father died, Attia Hosain was only eleven years old. They were a family of five children, the youngest born two months after the father's death, yet the mother took over all responsibility for them, and for the estate — an unusual step for a woman at that time — and brought up her children very strictly, according to tradition. Attia Hosain says "I learnt from her how strong women can be when faced with tragedy and pressure." Although she had English governesses and studied at the La Martiniere School for Girls, she had lessons in Urdu and Arabic when she returned home, and read the Quran, kept close to the roots of her own culture by her mother and, before her, by her father who made sure they never lost touch with their ancestral village. During his lifetime their house had been filled with the political leaders and great figures of the society of the time and "We seemed to live with the cultures of the East and the West in a way that was not dissimilar from that of many Indian families," but the daughters of the house had a traditional upbringing nevertheless, and lived sheltered, rather secluded lives. Their religious education was liberal and they did not wear *burqas* but the car had silk curtains at the windows!

Attia Hosain read "any books I could lay my hands on" and as her father owned an extensive library, she grew up — "unsupervised" — on the English classics. She went to the Isabella Thoburn College in Lucknow, then the foremost college for women in India, and won scholarships. She persuaded her mother she should not be kept at home with her sisters and was the first woman from a *taluqdar's* family to graduate — in 1933 — from the University of Lucknow. In spite of this not inconsiderable triumph, she resented the distinction made between sons and daughters in the family and the fact that she was not sent to Cambridge as her brother had been. Her rebellion took the form of a marriage to her cousin, against her mother's wishes. He had been educated at Clifton and at Cambridge. Her father-in-law was also a *taluqdar* and, like her father, played a prominent role in the political, civic and social life of the UP; he was Vice-Chancellor of the University of Lucknow.

The family tradition of weaving together the political and the intellectual strands influenced Attia Hosain's life and thought. She claims

I was greatly influenced in the 30s by the young friends and relations who came back from English schools and universities as left wing activists, Communists and Congress socialists. I was at the first Progressive Writers' Conference and could be called a "fellow traveller" at the time. I did not actively enter politics as I was (and may always have been?) tied and restricted in many ways by traditional bonds of duty to the family.

Her mother-in-law was right wing and represented the Muslim League in the UP Assembly but maintained her independent view that Muslim leaders should remain in India, not go to Pakistan, and look after the interests of Muslims in India. Attia Hosain confesses that her own ideal of womanhood was embodied in Sarojini Naidu, the poet/politician who made her "overcome my shyness and go to the All India Womens' Conference in Calcutta in 1933".

As a well-educated, thoughtful young woman at the heart of the storm in an India on the brink of Independence and Partition, she wrote for *The Pioneer*, then edited by Desmond Young, and for *The Statesman*, the leading English language newspaper in Calcutta. She also wrote short stories — "some published, some unpublished" — but "never believed in myself as a writer!" In spite of her ideals and those of many other Muslims in India, Partition proved inevitable at Independence and, rather than go to Pakistan, the Muslim ideal in which she did not believe, she chose to take her children to England, a country she had come to know when her husband was posted to the Indian High Commission, and earned her living by broadcasting and presenting her own women's programme on the Eastern Service of the BBC.

Events during and after Partition are to this day very painful to me. And now, in my old age, the strength of my roots is strong; it also causes pain, because it makes one a "stranger" everywhere in the deeper area of one's mind and spirit *except where one was born and brought up.*

To read her novel and short stories is to become aware of the many and varied threads that go to make up a rich and interesting life as well as the many doubts and struggles and contradictions it contained. They reflect her pride in ancestry and heredity as well as sorrow at the frequency with which they are tarnished by some heedless, unjust or selfish action. They present her ardent love for all that was gracious and splendid in the aristocracy she knew as well as her awareness of the dark obverse side experienced by hapless dependents. They show her keen sense of the two ruling concepts of Indian behaviour — *Izzat/* honour, and *Sharam/*dishonour — passionately adhering to the former and reworking in her mind the many forms taken by the latter, not always the tradi-

tional ones. They show her appreciation of the
warmth, supportiveness, laughter and emotional
richness to be found in the joint family as well as an
acknowledgment of how often the joint family could
become a prison and a punishment. She displays an
enormous pride and belief in womanhood but cre-
ates many, widely differing representatives of it, some
worthy of respect, others of pity, still others of shame.
The pleasures she takes in privilege and all its accou-
trement are never divorced from a sense of the responsibility of possessing them, an almost queenly
sense of *noblesse oblige*.

The many-coloured threads that go to weave the
matter of the two books on which Attia Hosain's
reputation is based also give a distinctive quality to
her prose. It is as rich and ornate as a piece of
brocade, or embroidery, resembling the sari she
describes in the short story "Time Is Unredeemable":
"deep-red Benares net with large gold flowers scattered all over it and formalised in two rows along the
edge as a border". Not for her the stripped and bare
simplicity of modern prose — that would not be in
keeping with the period — which might make it difficult for the modern reader not as at home as she
with the older literary style, but it is in harmony with
the material. It is also important to remember that
Attia Hosain is actually reproducing, whether consciously or not, the Persian literary style and manner-
isms she was taught when young, and reading her
prose brings one as close as it is possible, in the

English language, to the Urdu origins and the Persian inspiration. Urdu is a language that lends itself to the flamboyant and the poetic and so it is a suitable medium through which to describe the Muslim society of Lucknow and the Persian influence in north India, although married to the local Hindi of the Hindu population and modified by a Western education in the English language.

And the literary and the stylised are balanced by a certain delicacy and freshness as well as lightened by flashes of wit and humour. Her greatest strength lies in her ability to draw a rich, full portrait of her society — ignoring none of its many faults and cruelties, and capable of including not only men and women of immense power and privilege but, to an *equal* extent, the poor who laboured as their servants. Perhaps the most attractive aspect of her writing is the tenderness she shows for those who served her family, an empathy for a class not her own.

When this collection was first published, in 1953, John Connell described the short stories as "little vignettes, precise, loving and exquisitely true, in spirit and in fact," and the *Times Literary Supplement* noted their "unusual distinction and charm".

Exquisite, delicate, charming — unavoidable words when one attempts to describe the quality of Attia Hosain's prose. It is the literary equivalent of the miniature school of painting in India, introduced by the Moghuls. Her stories can well be likened to those busy little vignettes in gem-like colours (so often

actually including gems), of princes and princesses
sporting on moonlit terraces, rose gardens with foun-
tains and peacocks, bazaars with horse and elephant
carriages, peopled by lively, active figures all deeply
involved in a way of life, a period of time, a particular
place and age.

But there is more to them than their colour and
charm, their beauty and grace. What makes them
truly interesting is the reconstruction of a feudal
society and its depiction from the point of view of the
idealised, benevolent aristocrat who feels a sense of
duty and responsibility towards his dependents —
women as well as servants. This character is something of a stock-in-trade with writers about the Indian
scene of that period, but in Attia Hosain's work he —
or she — fades into the anonymous figure of the
narrator, and the interest is focused upon the lively
world of the servants and their families who live in
low-roofed, thatched mud huts in long rows in the
compound from where they can be summoned to
work at all hours. This is where the most intense
dramas take place, where the comedies and tragedies
are at their most heightened. Such aspects of poverty
as theft, prostitution, illness and exploitation are not
ignored but acknowledged as inherent in the social
structure and they are depicted with a vigorous real-
ism as well as warm compassion.

In this world of the servants' quarters and the compound, the main issues are exactly the same as in the
big house with its wealth and comforts. Chiefly, they

are the twin issues of *Izzat/Sharam*, honour/dishonour — in that world, at that time, a matter of life and death, quite literally.

In "The Loss", an aged maidservant, once wet nurse to the narrator, is robbed of all her savings, packed into a box under her bed. She is broken by the loss. " 'What am I, robbed of my possessions?' " she weeps. " 'I am destitute, a beggar, I am at the mercy of the lowest. What am I now that I should live?' " "What she had been yesterday, and the day before, and the day before that through the accepted years", replies the shocked narrator but, on reflecting upon her much mightier hoard of belongings, realises " 'What am I without mine?' " Determined to restore to the old woman what gives meaning to a lifetime of labour, she calls in her friend the police superintendent, to deal with the case, then is dismayed to learn that he suspects the old woman's son Chand who is known to have run up gambling debts. The narrator challenges Chand before all the servants who are trying to discover the thief by an age-old, time-tested method of making everyone chew a handful of rice to see in whose mouth the rice turns to dry powder (the fabricators of superstition could be psychologists) but the old woman will not let her son be put to the test. " 'What need have you to steal? God has given you enough. And if my son were to steal from me I would that he were dead, and I with him.' " Seeing that the loss of the family honour, *Izzat*, would be harder to bear than the loss of her belongings, the narrator

presses the matter no further. In their common re-
gard for *Izzat*, their common fear of *Sharam*, she finds
a link with the old woman as strong as when she was
an infant, the old woman her wet nurse.

In "White Leopard", a one-time dacoit, a brigand,
is zealous in protecting his *Izzat*, even if it is the
honour of thieves. He has given up a life of dacoity to
be a servant in a rich house, but boasts " 'Everyone
can't be like I was. Even these sons of mine . . . would
not make good dacoits. They are weak, credulous and
with no judgment. They cannot support a job; a job
must support them.' " But when one of those despi-
cable sons is accused of theft by his employer, Mr Bell
(once a shoemaker, Bela Ram, now a convert, a
Methodist, a shopkeeper, and despised both for his
origins and his duplicity), the father's reaction is
explosive and fierce — his Brahmin *Izzat* has been insulted by a low-caste shoemaker. " 'My son sells his
service, not his honour.' "

The other theme of these stories, and of their characters, high or low-born, is that of Kismet, fate, the
overruling belief that what is written into the palm of
the hand, spelt out by the stars in the sky, cannot be
altered or escaped and that it is the test of a human
being how he or she carries that burden, honourably
or with shame.

In "The Daughter-in-Law" an old maidservant goes
to the village to fetch the little girl who is married to
her son but not old enough to go to him as a bride;
articles begin to disappear from the house; the child

is suspected and found guilty of theft as well as other little crimes; her vacant look and stubborn silence broken by outbursts of senseless talk make the servants think of her as "possessed". The distraught mother-in-law wails " 'You talk as if you were certain she was a lunatic or possessed by the devil. Whatever she be, she is my kismet's burden; she must stay with me.' " Later, beleaguered by the others' demand that she be sent back to the village she accepts " 'Do with her what you will; she is my kismet's curse.' "

Still harsher is the story of the little girl in "The Street of the Moon" who is married off to an old, opium-addicted cook in the household. The women servants paint her hands with henna and rub her with jasmine-oil, preparing her for the wedding; Hasina is enchanted by all the fuss and laughs with delight, making her mother scold " 'Stop laughing, you shameless hussy. You will laugh even on your wedding day,' " and " 'Oh, what did I do to bear such a child?' " No sooner is the wedding over that the women scold " 'What does a man marry for? Just so the woman can sit and adorn herself? You are a poor man's daughter and a poor man's wife,' " and they make her change into her old rags and sweep the floor. Too high-spirited to be beaten into that, Hasina flirts with the younger men on the compound, even the old cook's son; when she is found out, she runs away. The old cook goes back to his old ways of taking opium and haunting the street of prostitutes in the bazaar and there finds her again.

Hasina's eyes looked into his, large black-painted, steel-bright, diamond-hard, from a powdered face pallid in the harsh light, with red-circled cheeks, and a straight-lipped, painted mouth set in a smile around tobacco-blackened teeth.

Those who inhabit the big house seem pale and ghostly by comparison with such characters, their lives have a thinness, a shrunkenness about them. In "The Gossamer Thread" the husband, a so-called "intellectual" fails his friend, a revolutionary, who asks for a night's shelter, because he is too cowardly to give it. Instead, his wife, an uneducated and simple woman who irritates him by her childishness, offers it readily. In "The First Party", a young bride is taken to a smart party in the Western manner, feels shocked by the behaviour and dress of the other guests and refuses to please her husband by dancing with them. More poignant is the once-pretty bride of "Time Is Unredeemable" who has grown old in her in-laws' home while waiting for her husband to return from his studies in England, delayed there by the war. When she learns he is to return, she takes the brave step of going into the city to buy "modern" clothes — a hideous coat she thinks will please him. He is not pleased, he is distressed — " 'I don't want you to wear that old coat, it reminds me of my landlady' " — and leaves her, unable to establish a relationship where none ever existed. Her life is wrecked. Kismet.

In this story, as in many others, "Westernisation" is seen as destructive of the old, traditional culture. The latter may be full of cruelties and injustices, but it is a pattern of life known and understood, therefore more acceptable and more fitting than an alien culture that has been neither fully understood nor assimilated. Attia Hosain's work is by no means an unreserved paean of praise for the old culture but is certainly full of an inherited, instinctive love for it.

Anita Desai, Massachusetts, 1988

PHOENIX FLED

EVERYONE who lived in the village and the hamlets nearby knew her. In their minds they associated her deathless years with the existence of their village. Both were facts accepted without question since the birth of consciousness.

She was so old she had become static in time, could never be older, had surely never been young. Her dry wrinkled skin was loose around the impatient skeleton. It enclosed her eyes in folds, hiding the yellowed cornea surrounding lustreless pupils. Yet there was vision enough to make her unconscious of its loss.

She used her withered hands for feeble grasping, her crooked fingers for uneasy touching, her bent legs for unsteady shuffling, and not her eyes but time's familiarity for seeing and recognising her changeless, circumscribed world.

Through the years the mud of the walls had not changed, the same wooden arches supported the same sloping thatched roof, the same doll's house sliced off a corner of the small courtyard. And the heavy wooden door leading outside creaked the same warning as it opened and the curtain of matting was lifted.

This was her complete world as she lay in the sun on her string bed—the walls, the arches, the thatch, the courtyard, the doll's house, the curtain, the door to the world outside.

That world had changed, quickening its step in noisy haste. As she lay on her bed, shrivelled lips moving in constant prayer, she heard the impatient sound of a car horn, and the distant desolate screech of an engine's whistle.

Sometimes that alien world stepped through the creaking door. A grandson, a granddaughter, a visitor from the city lifted the curtain. They were self-conscious as they bent towards her for her embrace, lowering their eyes, covering their heads, denying the world that violated her principles, where men and women walked and talked together. Her eyes were protectively dim to new stimuli, her ears dull to new sounds.

Yet they were bright and sharp when the great-grandchildren, the little ones, raced through the door. Then there was no conflict of worlds, they shared one created of their bright young love, not flat one-dimensional but given depth and form and colour by their curiosity, amusement and repulsion.

"How old, how old—and don't say it loudly—how ugly is Old Granny."

They would flap the loose hanging skin of her arm, lie on her lap and look, when she chewed an invisible cud, at the fascinating movement of her chin towards her nose, just missing it, then dropping down to begin again its upward drive. They would suddenly scream with high clear laughter, whirl around the bed, somersault to the floor and shout:

"Can you see us, Granny?"

"Of course, of course. An elephant has tiny eyes, but it can pick a needle off the ground."

"Can it, can it really? Tell us the story of the Elephant and the Needle, Granny."

When she walked, her back a broken spring, bent to the ground, they laughed.

"What are you looking for, Granny?"

"Looking at the ground into which I must go one day to look for the treasure that is buried there."

"Tell us of the buried treasure, Granny. Tell us a story."

That was their invisible bond, the common language they talked in their own private world. The daughters and sons, the granddaughters and grandsons stood outside it, deaf to its sounds, wrapped in their impatience and hostility, grudging dutiful affection to a parasitic old woman whom time refused to drop into releasing oblivion.

The visible bond between the old woman and the children was the doll's house. They loved it with the same passion. The children hung coloured glass globes in the tiny arches, dug twigs and grass into its small courtyard. Their gaily dressed rag dolls were propped on string beds under the thatch. She cleaned its mud walls with wet clay, her fingers following each curve and crevice with familiar affection. Their interest in it flamed high and burned low, but hers was as steady as her hold on life.

"Tell us a story, Granny."

She dipped into the deep well of her memories. She had no need to stretch in her effortless reaching to draw its constant treasure. The live past was always happily with her, the present an irritating dying burden.

The fly that sat on her nose a moment before was as forgotten as the reflex brushing it away, but her nose still twitched with the itching of the one that had sat on it seventy years ago.

Her mother said, "Don't sit there making such faces. The wind will blow on you and set your face for ever in that grimace. Kill the fly with your fan, can't you?"

Her mind telescoped life to make it possible for her weak old age to be sustained by the strength of her childhood. She was happy with the children, because she lived in their time.

The youngest one screwed up her face. "Granny, look at me, listen to me. I can whistle."

"Don't do that or the cold wind will blow on you and set your face in that grimace. Don't whistle or the soldiers will get you."

"Soldiers? Which soldiers?"

"The red-faced ones, like monkeys in red coats. They whistle to bad women. No village woman is safe when they pass by." Her aged body felt the fear of young girls when old women whispered:

"No woman is safe, no girl is safe."

"Oh, Granny," laughed the children. "How funny you are. The soldiers don't wear red coats, their clothes are dirty. And there are black-faced monkeys too. And they did not hurt us. They laughed and threw us sweets from their lorries."

"Don't eat their impure poison," she scolded. Then past memories lashed her present security. "Why," she quavered, "why did the soldiers come to the village?"

The children did not know, their elders did not care to tell. They could not find time from their own fears to reason why violence had changed its face, why they feared the departure of the soldiers as once she had feared their arrival.

The soldiers had driven into dust-clouds that billowed thick over the fields, thinning into an emptiness over distances that held a threat.

She did not feel it nor did the children, but the others lived heavily under its weight. The familiar stillness of their surroundings was an accomplice to their solace-seeking minds, as to hers. It could not come to them from out of known distances, to this village, these huts, themselves, the bestiality that was real only to their fear. The village lived uneasily, the breath of its life quickened or caught

13

when some outsider brought chill confirmation. Only Old Granny who had survived the threats of too many years refused to believe in its finality.

When the dread moment was upon them naked of their disguising hopes, they remembered only the urgency of their frenzied need to escape. Terror silenced the women's wails, tore their thoughts from possessions left behind; it smothered the children's whimpering and drove all words from men's tongues but Hurry, Hurry.

She refused to go with them. Her mind in its pendulum swing from their infecting fear to incredulity that neighbours should turn murderers rested always at one point. "I am old, I am feeble. I shall slow your flight. It is the children you must save. Besides," she added, drawing conviction from her years, "you will return. In the Mutiny we returned and our fears were more cruel than reality. Take care of yourselves, give my blessings to everyone in the Casbah. It is long since I went there, not since the wedding of . . ."

She sat on the string bed and looked at the door until all movement had ceased in the curtain before the creaking door now silent. Soon the outside air was stilled of all woeful noises. She looked around the disordered house, its beloved familiarity ebbing away. Near the doll's house sprawled a rag doll. She shuffled to it and propped it carefully in its proper place. Then she waited in silence, and suddenly whimpered like a lost child until she slept.

The creaking of the door woke her. She could not see who came, how many. She smelt the flaming thatch, and as shadows came nearer across the courtyard she tried to sit up.

"Mind," she scolded, pointing her bony finger, "mind you do not step on the doll's house."

THE FIRST PARTY

AFTER the dimness of the verandah, the be-wildering brightness of the room made her stumble against the unseen doorstep. Her nervous-ness edged towards panic, and the darkness seemed a forsaken friend, but her husband was already steadying her into the room.

"My wife," he said in English, and the alien sounds softened the awareness of this new rela-tionship.

The smiling, tall woman came towards them with outstretched hands and she put her own limply into the other's firm grasp.

"How d'you do?" said the woman.

"How d'you do?" said the fat man beside her.

"I am very well, thank you," she said in the low voice of an uncertain child repeating a lesson. Her shy glance avoided their eyes.

They turned to her husband, and in the warm current of their friendly ease she stood coldly self-conscious.

"I hope we are not too early," her husband said.

"Of course not; the others are late. Do sit down."

She sat on the edge of the big chair, her shoulders drooping, nervously pulling her sari over her head as the weight of its heavy gold embroidery pulled it back.

"What will you drink?" the fat man asked her.

"Nothing, thank you."

"Cigarette?"

"No, thank you."

Her husband and the tall woman were talking about her, she felt sure. Pinpoints of discomfort pricked her and she smiled to hide them.

The woman held a wineglass in one hand and a cigarette in the other. She wondered how it felt to hold a cigarette with such self-confidence; to flick the ash with such assurance. The woman had long nails, pointed and scarlet. She looked at her own — unpainted, cut carefully short — wondering how anyone could eat, work, wash with those claws dipped in blood. She drew her sari over her hands, covering her rings and bracelets, noticing the other's bare wrists, like a widow's.

"Shy little thing, isn't she, but charming," said the woman as if soothing a frightened child.

"She'll get over it soon. Give me time," her husband laughed. She heard him and blushed, wishing to be left unobserved and grateful for the diversion when other guests came in.

She did not know whether she was meant to stand up when they were being introduced, and shifted uneasily in the chair, half rising; but her husband came and stood by her, and by the pressure of his hand on her shoulder she knew she must remain sitting.

She was glad when polite formality ended and they forgot her for their drinks, their cigarettes, their talk and laughter. She shrank into her chair, lonely in her strangeness yet dreading approach. She felt curious eyes on her and her discomfort multiplied them. When anyone came and sat by her she smiled in cold defence, uncertainty seeking refuge in silence, and her brief answers crippled conversation. She found the bi-lingual patchwork distracting, and its pattern, familiar to others, with allusions and references unrelated to her own experiences, was distressingly obscure. Overheard light chatter appealing to her woman's mind brought no relief of understanding. Their different stresses made even talk of dress and appearance sound unfamiliar. She could not understand the importance of relating clothes to time and place and not just occasion; nor their preoccupation with limbs and bodies, which should be covered, and not face and features alone. They made problems about things she took for granted.

Her bright rich clothes and heavy jewellery oppressed her when she saw the simplicity of their clothes. She wished she had not dressed so, even if it was the custom, because no one seemed to care

for customs, or even know them, and looked at
her as if she were an object on display. Her discomfort changed to uneasy defiance, and she
stared at the strange creatures around her. But
her swift eyes slipped away in timid shyness if they
met another's.

Her husband came at intervals that grew longer
with a few gay words, or a friend to whom he
proudly presented "My wife." She noticed the
never-empty glass in his hand, and the smell of
his breath, and from shock and distress she turned
to disgust and anger. It was wicked, it was sinful
to drink, and she could not forgive him.

She could not make herself smile any more but
no one noticed and their unconcern soured her
anger. She did not want to be disturbed and was
tired of the persistent "Will you have a drink?",
"What will you drink?", "Sure you won't
drink?" It seemed they objected to her not drinking, and she was confused by this reversal of
values. She asked for a glass of orange juice and
used it as protection, putting it to her lips when
anyone came near.

They were eating now, helping themselves
from the table by the wall. She did not want to
leave her chair, and wondered if it was wrong and
they would notice she was not eating. In her confusion she saw a girl coming towards her, carrying
a small tray. She sat up stiffly and took the
proffered plate with a smile.

"Do help yourself," the girl said and bent forward. Her light sari slipped from her shoulder and the tight red silk blouse outlined each high breast. She pulled her own sari closer round her, blushing. The girl, unaware, said, "Try this sandwich, and the olives are good."

She had never seen an olive before but did not want to admit it, and when she put it in her mouth she wanted to spit it out. When no one was looking, she slipped it under her chair, then felt sure someone had seen her and would find it.

The room closed in on her with its noise and smoke. There was now the added harsh clamour of music from the radiogram. She watched, fascinated, the movement of the machine as it changed records; but she hated the shrieking and moaning and discordant noises it hurled at her. A girl walked up to it and started singing, swaying her hips. The bare flesh of her body showed through the thin net of her drapery below the high line of her short tight bodice.

She felt angry again. The disgusting, shameless hussies, bold and free with men, their clothes adorning nakedness not hiding it, with their painted false mouths, that short hair that looked like the mad woman's whose hair was cropped to stop her pulling it out.

She fed her resentment with every possible fault her mind could seize on, and she tried to deny her lonely unhappiness with contempt and

20

moral passion. These women who were her own kind, yet not so, were wicked, contemptible, grotesque mimics of the foreign ones among them for whom she felt no hatred because from them she expected nothing better.

She wanted to break those records, the noise from which they called music.

A few couples began to dance when they had rolled aside the carpet. She felt a sick horror at the way the men held the women, at the closeness of their bodies, their vulgar suggestive movements. That surely was the extreme limit of what was possible in the presence of others. Her mother had nearly died in childbirth and not moaned lest the men outside hear her voice, and she, her child, had to see this exhibition of . . . her outraged modesty put a leash on her thoughts.

This was an assault on the basic precept by which her convictions were shaped, her life was controlled. Not against touch alone, but sound and sight, had barriers been raised against man's desire.

A man came and asked her to dance and she shrank back in horror, shaking her head. Her husband saw her and called out as he danced, "Come on, don't be shy; you'll soon learn."

She felt a flame of anger as she looked at him, and kept on shaking her head until the man left her, surprised by the violence of her refusal. She saw him dancing with another girl and knew they must be talking about her, because they looked towards her and smiled.

She was trembling with the violent complexity of her feelings, of anger, hatred, jealousy and bewilderment, when her husband walked up to her and pulled her affectionately by the hand.

"Get up. I'll teach you myself."

She gripped her chair as she struggled, and the violence of her voice through clenched teeth, "Leave me alone," made him drop her hand with shocked surprise as the laughter left his face. She noticed his quick embarrassed glance round the room, then the hard anger of his eyes as he left her without a word. He laughed more gaily when he joined the others, to drown that moment's silence, but it enclosed her in dreary emptiness.

She had been so sure of herself in her contempt and her anger, confident of the righteousness of her beliefs, deep-based on generation-old foundations. When she had seen them being attacked, in her mind they remained indestructible, and her anger had been a sign of faith; but now she saw her husband was one of the destroyers; and yet she knew that above all others was the belief that her life must be one with his. In confusion and despair she was surrounded by ruins.

She longed for the sanctuary of the walled home from which marriage had promised an adventurous escape. Each restricting rule became a

guiding stone marking a safe path through un-
known dangers.

The tall woman came and sat beside her and
with affection put her hand on her head.

"Tired, child?" The compassion of her voice
and eyes was unbearable.

She got up and ran to the verandah, put her
head against a pillar and wet it with her tears.

THE STREET OF THE MOON

KALLOO the cook had worked for the family for more years than he could remember. He had started as the cook's help, washing dishes, grinding the spices and running errands. When the old cook died of an overdose of opium Kalloo inherited both his job and his taste for opium. His inherent laziness fed by the enervating influence of the drug kept him working for his inadequate pay, because he lacked the energy and the courage to give notice and look for work elsewhere. Moreover, his emotions had grown roots through the years, and he was emotionally attached to the family. He had watched with affectionate interest the birth, childhood, youth and manhood of the sons of the house and felt he was an elder brother.

Of his own age he was uncertain but felt young enough when opium-inspired. Eyes outlined with powdered 'soorma', tiny attar-soaked bit of cotton hidden in his ear, his cotton embroidered cap set at an angle, he went of an evening to the Street of the Moon.

The morning after he would be slower of movement than usual, and when he weighed the flour, the lentils, the rice and fat for the day his hands would shake, and Mughlani, who had charge of the stores, would shake her grey head and wheeze asthmatically: "You men, you are all animals even when your feet hang in the grave. What you need, Kalloo Mian, is a wife to keep you at home."

"What I need is someone to help me in the kitchen. It is hard work that makes my hands shake and my head grow heavy," he would grumble. But the repeated suggestion took root in his mind and he brooded over the need to find himself a wife. He had been married once when very young, but his wife had died and left him a son who had been nothing but a source of trouble.

Young Munnay lived with his mother's people and every now and again appeared saying he had lost his job and needed money. Kalloo would storm: "Where do you think I can find the money? Dig it from the ground? Pluck it from the trees? Wait for it to rain from heaven? Why do you not work, you shiftless wretch? Work here with me and I'll teach you to be a cook. I could get you three or four rupees a month as my help. That is how I started."

"Oh no," the boy mocked. "Start as your help and end as you have done! What great fortune have you piled up? I know the Collector Sahib's khansama who gets sixty rupees a month, and has a help, and you get twenty rupees like a plain barvarchi. I'll find work in a shop again, and be able to give you three or four rupees a month myself."

"Much you have given me already. Get away from here you lazy son of an owl," he raged, but he felt the sting of the taunts. He was not a plain 'barvarchi' who knew only how to cook Indian food, he was a 'khansama' who could serve the best English dishes too. Twenty rupees a month— why he could get sixty rupees too. He counted the number of people for whom he cooked—Khan Sahib one, Begum Sahib two, the two sons, guests, any number, say at least three or four a day, that made seven or eight. Then the servants . . . there was Mughlani one, and the widow Naseera who helped her, two—no one to help him—Nuru the bearer, three—Khan Sahib's bearer, four—his son Husnoo who worked for the master's two sons, five, himself, six, and of course the guests brought servants. That was much over twelve people— might be twice twelve meals a day for twenty rupees a month. One day he would ask for more pay or say, "I can find work anywhere, I can cook English food—"

But the day was not today, not tomorrow. . . .

Kalloo lived his drugged life in the smoke and heat of the kitchen, went each morning to the bazaar, haggled with the stall-keepers as he had haggled since his youth, returned to arguments with the Begum Sahib when she wrote the accounts, and then to his cooking. Sometimes he wished he had a wife to press his aching feet, his tired body.

When Naseera went home for a few days he hardly noticed it; one person less to cook for made hardly any difference to his work. But Naseera brought back her daughter. It caused quite a stir in the household. No one ever really thought of Naseera as a living woman. She was a humble ugly shadow moving and working as others ordered, dominated completely by Mughlani. And now her daughter had brought her to life for the brief period curiosity lasted that Naseera could have borne such a child as Hasina.

Kalloo grumbled : "One more mouth to feed. And will I be given enough stores? Oh no. I must be a magician."

Naseera when she came to the kitchen was apologetic. "Kalloo Mian, I had to bring her or she would have been ruined in the village. She will be no trouble. I've asked Begum Sahib's permission. She will help you, and all I ask for is a little food that can be spared and some old clothes. But I am growing old, and needed someone to care for me too."

"I know, I know, sister. I have a son, but worthless, curse him. And when one cooks for twenty, then what is it to add one more?"

"God be with you, Kalloo Mian, a widow's blessings on your head."

Kalloo wiped his eyes with his sleeve as he

peeled the onions and laughed: "I'll make her peel onions."

Next morning Mughlani grumbled as Kalloo weighed the rice. "Curse of my life. What can I do with her? Naseera wants me to train her. A grown girl like her is fit to be a mother, and what does she do? Sit all day admiring herself, being rude to her mother. Can she hold a needle? No. Can she cook? No. I said to Naseera, 'Your in-laws, did they think they were Rajahs and Ranis that they spoiled her so? Who will marry her for all her fine looks? Is she to sit like a Begum in some poor man's house, and will her mother-in-law do her work for her?' Blind fools. I'll teach her now what's what, the little hussy. She'll learn to sew in the daytime, sitting beside me, and I'll have my slipper handy. And in the evenings, Kalloo Mian, she'll sit in your kitchen, wash the dishes, grind the spices and watch you cook—I'll teach her if I have to kill her. . . ."

"You are very wise, Mughlaniji. Look at my son, the young rascal. These young people nowadays have new ideas, and no respect for their elders."

He picked up the tray, heavy with the heaped cereals, and went into the kitchen, lost in its smoky shadows for the day.

He was busy lighting the fire when she came. "Khansamaji," she called from the door, "Begum Sahib wants you to give the accounts now. She has to go out, so please hurry." He could see her slight figure outlined in the doorway.

"I'll be coming, I'll be coming—can't you see I'm busy?'

"What do I care? I only told you what she said, so don't you growl at me." She laughed merrily and was gone.

"No respect for her elders," he muttered as he reached for his cap and shoes.

She came in with fresh leaves of 'pān' while he was half-way through with the accounts. She sat on the steps at the far end of the verandah cleaning and drying each leaf as she put it in the silver container.

"Two rupees for eggs? Why so much?" frowned the Begum. Hasina's eyes mocked him.

"I charge only for what I use, and I use what is eaten at table. I don't eat eggs," he said with goaded defiance.

There was a moment's silence of surprise.

"But you do eat meat, and if that is the best you can cook you will have to be taught again. Day after day it becomes worse, swimming in water, no ghee at all. What becomes of the ghee you take? Let me see now, a quarter of a seer for the meat dish alone—" Over the Begum's bent head he could see the girl. She was hiding her mouth with her 'dupatta', but her eyes were dancing with cruel mirth.

He spluttered: "I do my best. I'm no thief—

29

I'm a slave; just a slave. I'm getting blind through cooking all day—all by myself with no one to help, and all for a miserable pittance. I could get three times as much anywhere else but I stay here because it's like my own family, and what do I get for it? I'm called a thief."

"Really! Have you taken leave of your senses? Control yourself! Go now, and come back when you have had less opium." The Begum stormed.

He did not look up as he stumbled out in case he saw the girl laughing at him.

In the days that followed he made her work harder, doing all the most unpleasant work. He would scold her and get Mughlani to scold her. She would mock him, and tease him and reply insolently. He roused even Naseera to beat her.

"She does no work. All she does is stand and roll her eyes at the young men, especially Husnoo," he told Naseera.

Husnoo was young and wore a turban with a high starched plume. On the green band across it was pinned the silver crest of his masters. He smoked their cigarettes, learned from them a few words of English. He was a man to break a village girl's heart. Hasina had seen only the men of her village, rough and earthy, marked by their hard struggle with the soil. When she was eleven she was made to stay in the cottage and not to see or talk to strange men. She was intoxicated by her new opportunities.

"Will you bring shame on my grey head?"
Naseera cried as she beat her. "Don't let me catch
you talking to any man but Kalloo Mian or I'll
burn your tongue with a live coal."

Hasina's eyes burned Kalloo with their angry
hate. He was haunted by her eyes. They shone
with bright black mischief normally, and the
thick outlines of 'kajal' made them too large for
her thin face. Her dark skin shone smooth, tight
stretched over her high cheek-bones. The small
gold ring in her nose danced above her small
mouth when she laughed at him. When she lifted
her arm to wipe the sweat from her brow and her
'dupatta' was displaced he could see the outline of
her firm young breasts under her thin shirt.

He went every evening to the Street of the
Moon. He dulled his senses with opium. Inevitably the whole household was affected.

At last Mughlani said to him: "This cannot go
on, Kalloo Mian. Everybody's anger is heaped on
my head through Begum Sahib. They won't turn
you out—for all their fine words about you being
too old a servant. The truth is, where could they
find anyone to work so much for so little? But I
have told her what is the cure. You must be
married, Kalloo Mian, and I have found you a
wife. I shall talk about it today, and let you know
tomorrow."

"Leave me alone. I want none of your schem-
ing." He shuffled off red-eyed and scowling.

31

In the evening Mughlani came to the kitchen. "Out of here, Hasina—go to your mother."

Hasina put away the large plate of rice she was cleaning, and skipped joyfully to the door, grinning at Kalloo: "Now you can do it for yourself."

Mughlani sat down on the low stool, and fanned herself with her small fan of plaited bamboo shoots which she had edged with frills of green silk.

"Kalloo Mian—listen carefully. I have spoken to Begum Sahib about your marriage. And we have decided in our minds what must be done. You must be married. And we have decided whom you must marry. Who else will marry the girl? She will have no dowry and she is no houri so she will not find a husband easily. And she is of an age when she must marry, or mark my words, there will be trouble.

"We have spoken to Naseera, and if you agree we will begin to make necessary arrangements. You must agree. We have decided you must marry Hasina."

Kalloo clutched the table for support, and wiped the sweat from his face. He lowered his eyes in sudden shyness and whispered, "I am the Begum's servant, and you are as my mother to me. I cannot but obey."

Preparations for the wedding toned the slack eventless atmosphere of the household. Mughlani appointed herself Kalloo's representative in all consultations, while the Begum Sahib looked after the interests of the bride.

Kalloo had a hundred rupees hidden in a box with a few pieces of his first wife's jewellery. He said he could get a loan of another couple of hundred, and pay it back gradually. The sons of the house said they would make his clothes for the wedding, and the bridal feast would be given by them. Mughlani said, "Now let me see what jewellery you have, and what we must have made. Everyone knows you are not a rich man so there will be no unnecessary ceremonies, no extravagance. But it is no pauper's wedding, and I will show what I can do, as if it were my own son's wedding—but alas! God gave me no children and He knows best." She wiped her tears in the corner of her 'dupatta', then busied herself with the jewellery.

"Silver anklets, nice heavy ones, rings for the feet—six bangles—you can get six more, they won't cost much and will look nicer—chain for the neck—you must get a necklace, a ring, something for the head, and don't forget the nose ring. We must not give her new ideas right from the start. When I was married, and her mother was married, we had nose rings. Everything else can be silver, but that must be gold. Never fear, I'll not spend too much money."

He lied to her, and borrowed more money

because he wanted to get his bride all she could desire.

He stopped going to the Street of the Moon. He had no time. When he was not working he was buying all that Mughlani told him to get. She went with him herself to buy the cloth for the bridal dress, the tinsel and gilt lace. She sat behind the drawn curtains of the 'ekka' while he went into the shops and brought materials out for her approval before he bought them.

He caught occasional distant glimpses of Hasina. Since the day of their engagement she was not permitted to see him or talk to him. She sat near her mother or Mughlani and had to hang her head shyly if her marriage was mentioned. She did not do so at first, but her mother had said she would be beaten if she were shameless.

Mughlani said, "In my days we didn't leave the room for forty days."

"Not so many surely," Naseera said mildly.

"As near as not to matter," Mughlani asserted. "And one was massaged with sweet-smelling ointments. Then on her wedding day the bride's skin was tight and scented. What do they care about it now? The rich go prancing around to the last day as shameless as the Angrez they copy, and the poor copy the rich. In my day they even taught us to cry when the Kazi asked, 'Do you give your consent?' Like this," and she wailed a repeated high-pitched descending scale. Hasina giggled and her eyes danced.

"Stop laughing, you shameless hussy. You will laugh even on your wedding day," Mughlani scolded.

"Oh, what did I do to bear such a child?" Naseera wailed.

At last time had caught up with Kalloo's impatient desire. It was the day of the wedding. Kalloo had asked two of his friends to cook that day and the next. His son came on leave for the occasion, and Kalloo gave him the new clothes he had had made for him. "You wretched boy, you don't deserve them. I must make you look respectable though it make me poorer still."

"Ah, but you are not too poor for a new wife," the son mocked.

"Get out of my sight, you ill-mannered, ill-fated one." Kalloo's anger was ineffective, breaking through several layers of his mind's joy that day. He was the centre of all attention, he enjoyed the suggestive banter of his friends, and the anticipation of slaked desire.

Hasina was made to lie quietly in the specially screened verandah. Her mother said, "If you move without my permission I shall beat you. Do what you like tomorrow when you are a married woman, but spare me shame today." She had plucked henna leaves from the garden hedge and ground the leaves to a thick paste. When she put

35

it on her daughter's hands and feet, and carefully evened the edges, she cried a little.

Mughlani arranged the clothes she had sewn, with the jewels, on large wooden trays and covered them with bright-coloured cloths. She counted the few pots and pans the Begum had bought for the bride, and gave a final polish to the cheaply pretty tin-plated betel box. She had made a red silk cover for it, embroidered with flowers in gold thread taken from the Begum's sewing-basket.

"Naseera," she said, "I hope your ungrateful child knows how lucky she is. She is not going empty-handed to her husband, thanks to Begum Sahib's generosity."

Hasina wished she could see all the wonderful things she would soon possess. Specially the betel box. Now she could eat betel all day, her own, made by herself, and she would eat even tobacco —the tiny silver pellets the Begum ate. She would do as she pleased after she was married—that silly Kalloo, he was so funny, she would laugh at him all day.

Mughlani called, "Naseera, be careful with that henna, see it does not become black."

Naseera wiped away a tiny bit of the paste and Mughlani said, "That is enough. See how red it is already. The girl has plenty of heat in her body it seems," and she laughed suggestively.

Naseera washed away the paste, and on the

moist crumpled red skin she rubbed sweet-smelling jasmine oil. Hasina stared happily at her bridal feet and hands. Mughlani said with wise authority:

"Listen to me, child. You will be a woman soon and must behave well and with modesty. The Kazi will ask you three times whether you will marry Kalloo Mian. Now don't you be shameless, like these modern educated girls, and shout gleefully 'Yes.' Be modest and cry softly and say 'Hoon.' Then he will come back after asking the bridegroom and tell you you are married. Then you must cry loudly."

"Or I'll pinch you," added Naseera.

To Hasina the ceremony was a confused memory of sudden fearful excitement induced by the wailing of her mother, the curious women crowding around, the growing heat, the sharp pain of the thick nose ring being forced in, her cries of pain then and when her mother pinched her, whispering fiercely:

"Don't shame me now, they are all here, the Begum Sahib and her friends."

She cried herself to exhaustion. Mughlani fanned her and said, "Poor child—how much she feels it! Ladies, please go now and come back when I have dressed her."

Kalloo knew how to behave as a bridegroom. He sat through the ceremony with his head bowed and his red handkerchief covering his mouth.

His friends whispered and nudged when the ceremony had ended: "There you are now—ready for the night. With a young wife you'll need all your wits about you—and more. Have you asked the Hakim's advice?—he can give you something that will make you younger than your son."

He resented the reference to his son. The ill-mannered boy had said, "Wah, wah, my father, in that flowery silk achkan and cap, with a garland round your neck, you look handsome enough to gladden my new mother's heart."

"How dare you talk to me so disrespectfully," he had shouted, and the boy said with mock respect, "Forgive me, I meant no harm," and swaggered off in his new clothes, hair well oiled and curled, lips faintly red with betel juice, humming a marriage song. Someone shouted, teasing him, "Who is the bridegroom—you or your father?" He answered, laughing gaily, "Let the old have their day."

Hasina in spite of the temporary misery of her discomfort was happy to be the centre of attraction. This was much more exciting than make-believe games with her friends when they had, with elaborate ritual, married their dolls dressed in gay rags and paper jewels.

Mughlani remembered past days of grandeur and ceremonial, and prepared for the one ceremony on which she had insisted. Today she and

Naseera were more important than the Begum herself.

She dressed Hasina in the scarlet pyjamas she had sewn. Their broad flounced edge was gay with colours—diagonal stripes of yellow, green and purple, with every seam tinsel-covered. The red shirt was covered with gold stars she had embroidered, and on the edges of the red tinsel-edged 'dupatta' she had sewn narrow fringes of gold and silver threads. She cut some gold thread into fine powdery pieces, and covered Hasina's hair with it. Some fell on her cheeks and the olive skin was gold-flecked. The beauty of Hasina's youth lent its vitality to the cheap colour and glitter.

She put on the jewellery, and hung garlands of jasmine and 'bela' round her neck, and round her forehead tied a silver ribbon band from which hung streamers of flowers veiling her face and falling to her knees.

She lifted Hasina's henna-stained hands and put them over the girl's face.

"Naseera, go and call the ladies. Everything is prepared," she said as she settled herself against the big bolster, supporting the girl's limp body with its sagging flower-weighted head against her shoulder. Hasina was tired, sweat-covered, but delighted to be at last the traditional bride.

The Begum Sahib and her chattering curious friends crowded round the bride. Mughlani said

39

with important pride, "First Begum Sahib must see her face, then the others." She moved aside the veil of flowers, moved the shielding hands, and held up the girl's face. Hasina remembered the brides she had seen, and kept her eyes shut, and tried not to smile.

"Well, well, being a bride suits her. She looks quite pretty," and the Begum Sahib put five silver rupees into her hands. Mughlani took them and carefully put them aside for the final accounting.

One by one the ladies stepped forward. Again and again the veil was moved aside, the hands taken away from her face, the now single silver rupee given and taken.

"Who would imagine this is Naseera's child?"

"Kalloo is certainly lucky."

"Imagine at his age getting this bride!"

"What pretty clothes!"

"And what a lot of jewellery for a poor man's bride!"

"Even if it is silver it must have cost a lot."

"You certainly have done well by your servants."

"How did you manage it?"

"Oh, it is nothing really—Mughlani has planned everything cleverly and carefully."

"The poor girl looks tired."

"Nonsense. This is one day that cannot be repeated. She can bear it."

"She has no new-fangled ideas like you have."

"Don't say that, my dear. It is a catching disease."

"Let us go and look at the bridegroom now. They are eating the marriage dinner."

"The bridegroom—oh dear, the bridegroom—"

The laughter and the chatter drew away and left a pit of silence into which the spirit dropped. Naseera began to weep silently, and Hasina cried with sudden shaking sobs. Mughlani whispered, "Hush, child, hush." They prepared to take her to Kalloo's small room in the servants' quarters.

For Kalloo the outward forms of a bridegroom's splendour lasted barely two days. He returned to work, and shed with his silk 'achkan' all visible signs of the eminence that had been so briefly his.

Within him was the restless drive of his unquenched desire. Hasina's tears and first reaction of resistance to every physical advance he made was followed by unwilling acceptance. He cared little for either, but resented her mocking laughter. Long days of work and sleepless nights left their mark, and his friends made a point of remarking on it. He could not even pretend to enjoy their banter, because he brooded over Hasina's cruel mockery.

Hasina enjoyed for a longer period her luxury of idleness, and her possessions. She accepted with fatalism the unpleasant price she paid for them with her unwilling body, but the days were

41

sufficiently long to prepare her for the nights and to forget them.

After a few days of admiring herself in the mirror that Kalloo's son had bought for her and hung on the wall where the light from the small barred window fell on it, of sitting at her mother's insistence shyly bridelike for hours beside the Begum or Mughlani, of lying on her bed waiting for Kalloo to sleep while she forgot his presence with thoughts of the clothes she would wear the next day, she was suddenly dragged back to reality.

Kalloo had built a fence of bamboo to screen off a small square space in front of the room allotted to them in the long low-roofed line of rooms for the servants. She could drag out their string bed on hot nights, or sit on it when the sun was not too hot, or in the cool evenings.

Mughlani came to see her one day: "Gracious, child—look at this place! Have you ever swept it? Now come on—off with those clothes—I made you enough workaday ones—take a broom and sweep the place. You are a married woman now, and must learn to keep your house clean."

It was a step from that to having once again to help her husband in the kitchen.

"And what does a man marry for? Just so the woman can sit and admire herself? You are a poor woman's daughter, and a poor man's wife," scolded her mother.

42

"There is work to be done in the house. You must help me, and your mother," admonished Mughlani.

Her clothes were blackened in the kitchen, her pyjama edges soiled with the dust of the swept floors, her jewels became heavy in the heat of work, and she gradually wore less and less. Only her 'dupattas' remained gay with bright colours. But after a time she was too tired to dye them, and wore them until their colours faded.

Her eyes lost their mischievous sparkle. Kalloo found she mocked him less, but lost her temper more.

Two months after her wedding day she first felt the sickness and listlessness that grew with each day. Mughlani was quick to notice it.

"Naseera—you are to be a grandmother," she said happily.

Naseera smiled. "God's will be done."

Kalloo was happy when he heard the news. He was pleased when the men joked, "Well, well, Kalloo Mian—you are a young man after all. Perhaps we should all get young wives."

Kalloo wanted Hasina to be careful. He would not let her help him in the kitchen. He sent for his son. "You said you wanted to leave your job after a month as your master was going to the hills. Well, leave it now, and come here and help me. I shall ask Begum Sahib to give you a few rupees and your food. If she refuses I'll tell her I'll leave.

43

After all, I don't get the pay I should get." Kalloo was suddenly determined and courageous. But he was surprised at his son's submissive acquiescence.

Hasina welcomed her reprieve. She rested and let Munnay do all the work. She went to help her mother and Mughlani, but they were careful that she should not strain herself.

Her eyes sparkled again. She took out her jewels and her bright clothes. Her skin stretched tight and glistening over the growing roundness of her body. Her breasts pressed outwards against her shirt and could barely be hidden by her 'dupatta.'

Kalloo was happy. His son seemed happy and grew daily more hard-working. His wife was more acquiescent and did not quarrel. What if occasionally the mockery returned to her eyes and laughter?

It was some time before he became conscious of the strange way his friends looked at him; their sudden silences when he came in as they were talking, not knowing he was near. He was uneasy, and lost his placidity. When Mughlani conveyed to him the Begum's message that the food was poorly cooked he did not ignore it with his usual remark, "Nothing will please her—she wants a lot in return for a little," but he flared, "Tell her to find another cook. My son and I work well enough. I am not a slave that I sell my son in bondage with myself."

Mughlani said slowly, troubled by asthma and

embarrassment, "Your son—Kalloo—it's none of my business really—but can you not find someone else to help? Your son is young and strong, and can find better work surely."

"And why should I?" he said aggressively. "He works well enough for me and has changed his habits, God be thanked. Besides, Mughlaniji, can you—or the Begum Sahib for that matter— find someone to work for so little?"

"Kalloo Mian, I said nothing really. Who am I? Just an old woman. But youth is a strange and dangerous thing. Hasina is very young."

"Hasina? Why do you talk of Hasina?"

"It is nothing, nothing, Kalloo Mian. Come on, weigh the rice, I haven't the whole day to spare."

Into Kalloo's slow-thinking mind the poison drop of Mughlani's suggestion worked its corrosive destruction. He watched his son carefully when he was with Hasina, found new meaning in their happy laughter, their easy acceptance of each other's presence. Between him and Hasina when alone there were veils of long silences torn by his compulsive desire, but since his son was with them she was pleasant, thoughtful of his comfort. He had not thought it strange till now. What made her change? Who made her change? The baby she was to bear him, of course. But why then did he sense the pity, the gibes, the laughter in the sudden silences of his friends?

He had always done the shopping himself,

trusting his son neither with money nor with judgment to choose well. It kept him away two hours in the mornings—he had to go very early; and very often he was out for an hour or so in the evening. He noticed his son seemed to have lost his love of wandering.

"Munnay," he said one day, "I want you to go to the bazaar from now on. I do not feel too well, and you must learn to do this work too."

His quickened perceptions noticed the look of dismay on his son's face. Hasina was behind him, but there was a sharp note in her voice when she said, "What is wrong with you suddenly? You look well enough."

"I did not ask your opinion," he said angrily.

"It would be better if you did. What do I care who goes shopping? I was thinking only of Begum Sahib, and the accounts if anything goes wrong."

"And why should it? He is no suckling babe in arms." He walked out and beyond the bamboo fence, but stood at one side waiting. After a few moments Munnay came out. He saw his father and started with surprise, stopped the fraction of a moment, then whistling loudly walked towards the kitchen. Kalloo went back to his room. He thought he saw Hasina draw quickly back from the door. When he went in she was lazily combing her hair. He shut the door. She said angrily, "What do you want?" Then with revulsion— "No, not now, not now." He bolted the door.

He was careful in the presence of his friends and the other servants of the household that they should notice no change in his behaviour. But he planned his days so that Hasina was not alone with Munnay for more than unavoidable moments of time. He noticed her restlessness and increasing fits of bad temper, she became careless about her appearance, and her face lost its roundness. Naseera and Mughlani said it was natural with a first baby, and that it must be a girl to give her so much trouble carrying it.

His son was sullen, and his old insolence was creeping back. His work became careless. Kalloo threatened to send him away, and noticed with alarm the threat strangely made him work better. He had overlooked mistakes in the shopping, even taken the blame when accounts were wrong, and made them up with cuts from his meagre salary. He was determined not to leave the two alone for so many hours. Now he used his threat effectively, "Either you be careful with the shopping, or I shall throw you out of the house."

The torment of his suspicions increased with each day of his isolating silence. He took very little opium now to be more alert. Hasina and he slept in the room since Munnay had come, and let him sleep in the small screened space. She complained bitterly of the stuffiness, and made him open the door before he went to sleep. He slept now with

47

a wakeful watchfulness that exhausted him after a long day's hard work.

After some days he found himself consciously fighting against the strong desire to sleep, and was not surprised to find it a losing battle. There followed nights when he slept deeply unconscious. He became suspicious, particularly as Hasina seemed better tempered and Munnay worked better.

One morning Kalloo woke to find it broad daylight. He was a very early riser, and his first reaction was of shock and fear that he was late for work. Then he saw Hasina's anxious face, and heard the relief in her voice: "So you are awake at last? I was worried, and got the stores for you from Mughlani."

He pushed her aside and went to the tap outside to wash, already thinking of the replies he would give to questions about his late rising. But his suspicions kept pushing through all other thoughts.

When Hasina had gone to the house to help her mother he went to his room and searched in his box where he kept his opium. His fears were reality. She must have been doping him every night and had been careless and given him more than usual the night before. How did she do it? he wondered, and his slow mind saw the obvious. In the betel she usually gave him every night.

That night he put the betel into his mouth, but walked outside and spat it out behind the fence.

He replaced it with one he had made for himself, and went back.

Some time after he lay as if in deep sleep he felt her sit up and her breath was upon his face. He kept his eyes shut, and breathed evenly. She got up, and he heard her go outside. He heard their voices outside in soft smothered whispers. He heard Munnay's bed creak with her body's added weight. His eyes were wide open and unseeing, and his suddenly heavy body was rigid on his bed. He tore himself from the bonds of his horror and staggered to the door. They must have heard him for Munnay was crouched at the far end of the bed staring with frightened animal eyes, and she was curled up with her 'dupatta' wrapped tight over her head, hiding her face and shielding her body from blows. Kalloo's body was quivering, and he leant against the wall for support. His horror and anger were overshadowed by a deep shame. The silence of the night was an enemy turning each whisper of his shame into a shout of proclamation. Any minute the whole household would be awake and mocking him.

He whispered hoarsely, "Come inside"—and stumbled in. They followed him silently, not daring to look at him. He said, forcing his voice low, "I cannot kill you as I would—I cannot even proclaim your shame by cutting off her nose and turning her on the streets because it is my shame. Now get out of here before I—" He choked, and tears covered his ravaged face. Munnay moved silently to the corner where he kept his tin box. His frightened eyes stared at his father as he picked it up and went out of the door. Hasina sobbed silently, her face still covered. Kalloo stood listening as his son moved in the courtyard, wrapping his bedding.

In the deep silence before dawn he could hear Munnay's bare feet on the dusty path beyond the fence, and wondered who else was awakened by the noise. There were no sounds but of Hasina's crying. He lay on the bed, turned to the wall, and it seemed the sobs that tore his throat twisted his stomach.

In the morning the others noticed Munnay's absence, but Kalloo's red eyes and swollen face silenced them. He said aggressively, "That wretched boy has run away again. He was never one for steady work."

Hasina lay all day with her face covered, and he said to Naseera, "You had better look after your daughter. She is not well."

Naseera felt the heavy burden of her daughter's shame and cried when no one was near. She said nothing to Hasina, but with her eyes accused her. Mughlani was mercifully silent.

Time inevitably levelled the emotional upheaval in their simple lives. The physical exhaustion of Kalloo's hard work tired his mind too much for him to brood on his betrayal. Hasina went back to the routine of her life. Her eyes had lost their softness, her mouth its upward curve, and her teeth were edged with the black stain of too many tobacco-flavoured betels. She had pushed girlhood aside.

She was beginning to feel the growing weight of the child within her and resented it. It was a relief to her, in spite of the extremity of the pain at the time, when she lost it after an accidental fall in the dark. Kalloo had even sent for a doctor when the midwife had given up hope. His grief was intense, and Naseera cried as if she herself had lost a child. Hasina enjoyed through illness once again the luxury of attention and idleness.

When she was strong enough to work her mother said to her, "I have spoken to Begum Sahib. I shall work in the kitchen, and you will do my work in the house."

Hasina could not hide her delight. More than the hard work of a kitchen-maid, she hated the constant curbing presence of her husband. She felt his eyes on her all the time. His negative gentleness irritated her.

She helped Mughlani and did her mother's work, but enjoyed most her work as the Begum's personal maid. She loved sensuously the feel of the silk clothes she pressed and folded. The silver, the perfumes, powder and paint arranged on the toilet table fascinated her. She had never before been allowed to touch anything in the room except by stealth. Now she was free, and not watched. Mughlani sat in the verandah most of the time, and the Begum was out quite a lot.

One of Hasina's duties was to make betels in the morning, and after meals arrange them with cloves and cardamom on a small silver tray and give it to Husnoo.

He was older than Munnay, but much better looking. The memory of his first disturbing impact on her consciousness was overlaid by the accumulated experiences of the interval between her fresh girlhood and her forcibly ripened womanhood. She was attracted by his deliberate seduction, different from the spontaneity of her relationship with Munnay. She was very careful at first, but time and her emotions made her forget the first unpleasant experience.

Her lost childish gaiety was replaced by a more sensual charm. She was conscious of herself as a woman.

Kalloo felt again the uneasiness of her strange good humour and acquiescence. He could not confirm his suspicions, and his nerves once again were frayed.

Mughlani had noticed Husnoo loitering around the inner rooms more than usual. She made a point of walking in suddenly, and sometimes saw him disappear while Hasina bent over some piece of work with suspicious care. Twice or thrice she caught them in laughing intimate conversation.

At last she said to Hasina, "You shameless girl —have you not learned your lesson? Why do you talk to strange men?"

"What harm do I do? Must I not talk or laugh at all? You people always think badly of me," and she cried, angry and afraid.

Mughlani said, "You will live to repent this. Kalloo should have kept you in purdah."

She felt it her duty to warn Kalloo, but he was powerless without proof against his wife's angry denials. In his perplexity he returned for solace to opium. It dulled the needle-points of resentment, but also dulled his senses, loosened the bonds of his body's enslavement. Hasina became a burden.

One afternoon he went into his room when she should have been working and was surprised to see her standing near the window. She was trying to catch the light as she looked into the mirror. She started guiltily as he came in, and drew into the shadows, drawing her pyjamas low to cover her feet.

He walked up to her, and pulled her round to face him as she turned away.

"What, by God and His prophet, have you got on your face?" he said in shocked surprise.

It was covered with a thick layer of powder, her cheeks were red-rouged, and her mouth daubed with lipstick.

"Where did you get that stuff from? Must you look like a woman of the bazaars as well as behave like one?"

53

She flared: "Begum Sahib uses it. You dare call her that."

"You are not the Begum Sahib. Leave the rich alone. Tell me, where did you get it?"

"She gave it to me."

"Tell me the truth, or I shall go and ask her."

"I took it. I'll put it back. I meant no harm. I wanted to see what it looked like," and she cried in sudden fright. She could not tell him Husnoo tortured her with his boastful stories of city women who adorned themselves in this new manner, excited him, made him feel a man of the world.

Kalloo felt a new courage now that the wrong was not done to him.

"And what are you hiding there?" He pulled up her pyjamas. She was wearing silk stockings.

"Allah," he said, and sat heavily on the bed. "Now you're a thief too. This I cannot stand. I've been here twenty years or more; I cannot have this shame on my head. What sin did I commit that fate brought you to me? What am I to do, you accursed wretch?"

She whispered with frightened repetition, "I'll put them back. No one will know. No one knows."

"But I shall go and tell. It is my duty to tell. I cannot have you wandering in the house, a thief."

"Please, I beg of you, I touch your feet. Don't tell. It will not happen again."

From that day Kalloo would not touch her. His

pride kept him silent, and to the world she was his wife, but to him she was his evil destiny. It was a relief to him when one morning he woke to find her gone. Husnoo had disappeared too.

Naseera cried with shame. Mughlani said, "I knew it. He should have kept her in purdah." Begum Sahib said, "The ungrateful wretch." Husnoo's father said, "She ruined my son, that street walker. I'll never let her keep him. Wait till he comes back to ask for money. He can't live on air for ever." Naseera cried, "May she die. To me she is dead already."

Kalloo did not wish to remember the tempestuous period of his life when Hasina became part of it. When Husnoo returned contrite and self-conscious after a month, and his father had got him back into service as a reward for his own long years of work, Kalloo bore him no grudge.

Naseera avoided him, and was sullen in his presence. Only Mughlani was able to satisfy the curiosity of the whole household. Hasina was working somewhere. Husnoo had found her the work when his money was nearly spent. He had left her because of his father's threats, and in any case why should he have married such a woman? Mughlani spared Kalloo's feelings and did not add the derisive "I am not as great a fool as Kalloo." But he visited her regularly and pretended he was the husband.

When Mughlani talked to him of Hasina,

55

Kalloo tried to appear uninterested. He would not look at her, and busied himself with his work. Sometimes he would force himself to comment, "She had an evil spirit in her. . . . Naseera bore a serpent." Once he even acknowledged the relationship his silence denied. "I am well rid of her."

He thought of her more and more as the days went by, and the hurt to his pride healed.

He missed her most when Mughlani stopped talking of her. There was no way of knowing what had happened to her. Husnoo had told Mughlani she had run away with someone without telling him.

She returned to his opium dreams as the innocent, gay, mischievous girl he had desired and married. He was obsessed by the image and was driven to seeking release in the Street of the Moon.

He found it one night as he looked up at the women sitting under the bright lamps smiling their invitations down to the anonymous darkness of the narrow crowded street. Hasina's eyes looked into his, large, black-painted, steel-bright, diamond-hard, from a powdered face pallid in the harsh light, with red-circled cheeks, and a straight-lipped painted mouth set in a smile around tobacco-blackened teeth.

He stared in unwilling recognition, then stumbled and ran down the street, away from that murderous face which had in a brief moment destroyed the long-enslaving image.

TIME IS UNREDEEMABLE

WHEN the second cable arrived, confirming the date he was to sail, Bano allowed herself to believe her husband was really coming back.

She was sitting in the thatched verandah sewing when her father-in-law came in. He held his spectacles in one hand, the cable in the other, and it trembled as if an unseen current caught it in the still air.

The women who observed purdah from him twittered like disturbed birds and hurried into the inner room.

"Read it to me," said her mother-in-law. "Tell me quickly what it says." In her agitation the red betel juice sprayed from her mouth.

Bano kept her head lowered as she tried to thread the needle. Her father-in-law put on his spectacles, pulled at his beard, pushed back his woollen cap, and held the cable close to his eyes.

"How long you take . . ." grumbled her mother-in-law. Bano could hear her own heart's echoes sound like a drum within her ears, and at the back of her head.

Her father-in-law cleared his throat, translated the words of the cable and added, "So, God willing, he will be home with us at the end of next month."

"The end of the month," sobbed her mother-in-law in her extremity of joy. "God be praised!"

Bano felt sharp points of tears press against her eyelids, but her habit-strengthened sense of propriety set a guard on her rebellious feelings, and her face was drained of emotion. Her mind, by its simplicity, reduced the complications of her thoughts, and her anxiety concentrated safely on external things as she wondered what her husband would look like after all these years, what he would think of her, what she would say to him, what she should wear when he first saw her. At the same time she responded to the sounds of the old couple's voices, picking key words to make them intelligible without breaking her own web of thought. Her mother-in-law made plans for immediate celebrations, her father-in-law for his son's future.

"What," sighed the old man, "will the boy do when others are already established? Ah, these years, these years destroyed!"

The sigh echoed mournfully in Bano's mind, and the chill of wasted years fell upon the formless future.

Her mother-in-law said, "Whatever is in his Kismet and hers must happen. Their life is beginning, and, for all I care, mine can end. I have lived nine years for this day."

Bano's father-in-law cleared his throat, blinked his eyes rapidly, and said, "I must be going. My game of chess is unfinished. . . ."

When he had gone the women crowded back, with so many questions to ask and opinions to express that one could not wait for another to begin a sentence or finish it, and their words formed a many-layered patchwork of sound obscuring Bano's silence.

Bano was sixteen when she was married to a reluctant Arshad a month before he sailed for England. In that brief, busy month she accepted the young stranger, barely two years older than herself, as the very focus of her being. To her mother and his the hurriedly arranged marriage was a moral insurance.

"To a mother of many girls both safety and wisdom counsel an early marriage," said her mother.

"If you push a boy into a sea of temptation will a hair of his head remain dry? Now he will not bring home a foreign woman," said Arshad's mother.

For two years after her marriage Bano's life was pleasant enough because there was no questioning of its circumscribed character. She was isolated from the outside world not only by physical seclusion but by mental oblivion. Arshad's letters came literally from a different world, yet both she and his mother were conscious only of the physical

59

separation of distance. He wrote regularly to his father about his studies, to his mother of his health. To Bano he wrote short, formal letters, but she was content, not expecting more. Sometimes he sent her postcards from countries he visited, and she showed them to her friends with a sense of vicarious pleasure as if she were worldly-wise by their possession.

Her father-in-law, who considered himself a man of liberal ideas, was pleased when Bano decided to learn English from his old friend Hari Ram's English wife. Of Mrs. Ram's shortcomings as a teacher, her dropped aitches, her ungrammatical colloquialisms, Bano was unaware; she was conscious only of the fact that Mrs. Ram could help her prove to Arshad that she was not like the other girls in the family, ignorant and old-fashioned.

Mrs. Ram lived in the small house next door, on the edge of penury. Her bleached, untidy, sagging appearance reflected her husband's failure as a lawyer, as a politician. They had settled in this small town after years of weary struggle to keep up appearances; and Mrs. Ram, who had always been familiar with poverty, welcomed its gentler nature. She was touched by Bano's affection, and grateful.

Bano lived her dutiful uneventful life, and was not unhappy.

Then the war broke out.

To Bano and her mother-in-law war meant nothing except in terms of Arshad's safety, and the despairing knowledge that he would not return until it ended.

In the winter of 1940 Mrs. Ram went away with her husband when he was given a good post in a new Government department. Bano put away her English books.

Without his friend Mr. Ram her father-in-law's loneliness increased his morbid anxieties about Arshad and the fate of his shaken world. He retired with his family to his ancestral village home.

Bano drew further away in time and space from Arshad; her only consciousness of it was that his infrequent letters took longer to arrive.

Endless years of waiting, of living the life of neither a wife nor a widow, pitied by her relatives, wept over by her mother and mother-in-law, hag-ridden by her misgivings that Arshad might die or marry again, wrung the spirit out of her.

The war ended.

The sharp sting of anticipation revived Bano; in her happiness there was a mysterious suggestiveness of an expectant bride, a radiance that lent her beauty and gentleness. She took out her English books again, and tried painfully to remember all she had forgotten, daring even to ask her father-in-law's help.

When Arshad wrote it was difficult to get a

61

passage and he would be indefinitely delayed, she was cast into a gloom which was as deep as the heights to which her joy had carried her. She was haunted by the suspicion that he did not wish to return, that he had found a woman. Then the habit of acceptance closed around her, obliterating all peaks of feeling, and she waited once again for the news that would clear this mist.

It came with the first cable, and was made real by the second.

Every breath and movement and thought now became a preparation of herself for the first moment of meeting Arshad. Above all else she wished to make him realise that she was not an ignorant girl of whom he, with his foreign education, need be ashamed.

Gradually a plan took shape in her mind: she would not even look like the other girls in the village, she would not wear the customary clothes no matter how much her mother-in-law insisted, she would wear a sari, new and modern. And a coat, not a shawl.

She confided in a favourite cousin who conveyed her wishes to her mother-in-law, as modesty forbade a direct approach in a matter which concerned her husband, however indirectly. The old lady, in her present mood of happiness, willingly gave her consent that Bano should go to the city to do her shopping.

Bano could think of no one more suitable than

Mrs. Ram to advise her, especially about the coat, which had to be of the latest English fashion, and asked her father-in-law to write and request Mrs. Ram to help her, not trusting her own unpractised English.

A visit to the city was a rare and exciting event, usually on the occasion of a wedding or celebration, sometimes because of a serious illness or death in the family, seldom for very special shopping. It called for a great deal of bustle and preparation.

Bano's father-in-law insisted on making all the arrangements himself, and said he would go with her because he wished to take this opportunity to meet his friends and discuss Arshad's future.

The day she was to leave the young girls in the house joked with Bano as if she were on her way to her wedding; they shared her excitement.

The tonga which was to drive them to the small country station for the first, bumping, dusty half-hour of the two-hour journey was drawn up near the door of the zenana. The bells on its harness rang gaily as the nondescript grey horse shook its head and flicked its tail to shake off the irritating flies. A sheet was tied round the back of the tonga and another to screen Bano from the driver, beside whom sat her father-in-law. Bano carried with her the shrouding 'burqa' she would wear to cross the platform.

When everything was ready for her to leave, the

elder women embraced her, the young girls came with her to the door, and everyone called out, "God protect you. God be with you."

When she arrived at their house in the city Bano did not tell her relatives much beyond this, that she had some shopping to do for her mother-in-law. Their expected banter about her husband's return she welcomed with simulated shyness.

After her father-in-law had rested, he told her he was going to see Mr. Ram, who lived some distance away in the Civil Lines. She asked him with a courage born of excited anxiety to tell Mrs. Ram to come for her as early as possible the next day as there was so little time and so much to do.

Next morning she was up early, and ready long before she expected Mrs. Ram to arrive. It seemed to her half the day was gone before she did come, though it was only ten o'clock.

Mrs. Ram looked no older, was stouter, and a gleam of prosperity glanced lightly over her faded face. After the first moments of affectionate greeting and questioning that closed the gap of separating years, she asked Bano what she wished to buy. Bano was embarrassed and hesitant in the presence of her relatives.

"A few clothes," she stammered.

"Ah," smiled Mrs. Ram with heavy coyness. "In preparation for Arshad's return! Well, well,

64

girls will be girls. But we must hurry, dear, as I'm ever so busy these days with parties and meetings."

When Bano brought her 'burqa' from her room, Mrs. Ram's pale eyes widened: "Surely, dear, you will not wear that?"

Bano looked at her relatives diffidently. "My father-in-law . . ." she began.

Mrs. Ram shrugged her shoulders, and looked with distaste at the shapeless garment.

In the car she said, "You must take it off when we get to the shop. It will attract ever so much attention, because no one that I know of wears it any more. And tell me, dear, exactly what you want to buy so that I can tell the driver where to go."

Bano said softly, "A sari, and a coat."

"I know just the right shop. All the best people go there; they know me well and it makes all the difference when things are hard to get."

Bano let herself drift on the stream of Mrs. Ram's will. As they drove through the narrow streets towards the wide avenues of the Civil Lines she removed the offending 'burqa' but was glad the closed car hid her from passers-by. She tried to explain as well as her restrictive shyness would permit her about the kind of coat she wanted, but what it meant to her was impossible to convey because it was a small part of all she had carried within herself for years.

"Do you want it for the evening or the day?"

That puzzled Bano, who did not know the difference.

"For all the time," she said.

"I see, a nice practical warm coat. How much do you wish to spend?"

She had not thought of details. "I have three hundred rupees altogether."

"That is not much really, seeing as prices are so high."

Bano looked with pained amazement at Mrs. Ram. Not since she was a bride when special clothes and jewels were necessary had she spent more on herself at one time; surely it was more than Mr. Ram had earned once. Mrs. Ram, enjoying this new experience of being depended upon, felt generously eager to please.

"Oh well, don't worry, dear, we'll manage."

In the shop Bano felt uncomfortably exposed to the glances of the strange men who served them. She nervously clutched the edge of her sari, with which she had covered her head and arms. Her self-consciousness made her unable to concentrate on the choice she had to make from the cloth that was unrolled in untidy heaps before her, and the saris that were piled around. She was glad to submit to Mrs. Ram's choice.

The sari that was chosen was of deep red Benares net with large gold flowers scattered over it and formalised in two rows along the edge as a border.

"Red for a bride," whispered Mrs. Ram with a meaning smile. For the blouse Mrs. Ram chose a piece of red satin, not exactly the same shade as the sari, but she considered it would not be noticed in the right light.

The coat presented a number of problems. There were none ready of the right size, the choice of materials was limited, and it would take three weeks to get it sewn.

"Not three weeks," said Mrs. Ram, "not when I order it. You'll get it ready in ten days."

"We do our best to please you, madam, but we can't promise. As for the cloth, as you know, madam, if you can't get it here you will not find it in any other shop."

Mrs. Ram nodded agreement. Among all those confident people Bano felt she knew nothing, and within her was a growing panic. She wanted to get away quickly. Suppose her father-in-law walked down the street and saw her without her 'burqa'?

She agreed happily when Mrs. Ram said, "Leave it to me. I'll choose the cloth."

"What about fittings?" said the solicitous salesman.

"What about the fittings?" mused Mrs. Ram. Bano looked lost in her puzzled ignorance.

Mrs. Ram felt expansively helpful: "Well, well, dear, leave it all to me. I'll buy the cloth, have it made up, and send it to you with one of my husband's orderlies. Send for your tailor," she ordered the salesman. "He can take the measurements, and I know he is good enough not to need a fitting. He does all my work, mine and Mr. Ram's, and the girls'."

Mrs. Ram rode high on the waves of authority, and Bano was overwhelmed. She did not like being measured by a strange man, but by now she was prepared for anything.

As they were leaving the shop a young woman in a sari walked in, unaware of Bano's curious glance. But in Bano's mind the impression of her face remained after it was out of sight. She blushed and said to Mrs. Ram, "Could you please buy me some powder, and colour for my lips? And please don't mention it to anyone."

"Lipstick and powder?" said Mrs. Ram, and she leant back, the folds of her face and chin shaking with affectionate amusement. "How our young Bano is changing!"

For some days after she returned to the village Bano carried within and around her the magic of the two-day visit to the city, then it merged into the growing excitement of Arshad's approaching arrival.

Mrs. Ram kept her promise and two weeks later the coat arrived. Bano felt a vague disappointment when she unpacked it, because in her imagination it was something wonderful; but she thought it must be right because Mrs. Ram had chosen it.

It was of heavy rough-surfaced material, maroon with faint flicks of grey, plain and belted. The sleeves pulled because it was somewhat narrow across the chest, and when buttoned was tight across the hips.

Her mother-in-law and other elders did not like it, preferring richer materials and more ornamentation, but they joked, "Perhaps this is what is worn now by memsahibs, and now that her husband is coming back a sahib she must wear it."

A week before Arshad was to return, welcoming relatives started arriving and soon the house was full. There were beds down the length of the thatched verandahs and in the rooms, and on them the women sat by day and slept at night.

Three extra women came as usual from the barber's family to help with the cooking; and the village songstresses, who sang in the zenanas, sang marriage songs every evening. The fat one, who was their leader and beat the rhythm on the long drum, started singing even the special suggestive songs, but Bano's mother-in-law stopped her.

The religious recital was to be on the day after Arshad was home, but for three days before, preparations were in full swing, and over a hundred guests were expected. Sweets were being prepared by the 'halwai' in a specially constructed shed in the outer courtyard, and in the zenana the

women cut betel nuts and prepared 'pãn', piling
the small green cones in baskets covered with
damp cloths. Bano's mother-in-law made a list of
all the kinsfolk, those who would come to the
'Milād' and those who could not, and to all of
whom the sweets must be distributed, each person
getting an equal portion. In a corner of the courtyard were collected the shallow pottery saucers to
hold the sweets.

Bano had no special importance in the general
pattern. She did whatever her mother-in-law
asked her to do.

A room that was easily accessible from the
men's part of the house was prepared for Bano and
Arshad, and she moved into it a day before his
return. The silver-covered ornamental legs of her
marriage bed were taken out of storage, and a
frame fitted on them. In the plain whitewashed
room the bed with its red satin counterpane
gleamed when the sun shone through the window,
and at night it was warm by lamplight.

Bano had hung muslin curtains on the windows
and doors, dyed a pale pink and tied with ribbon
bows; and on the table by the armchair she had
put her favourite vase, a woman's hand holding
up an ornamented cone coloured pink and blue.
She had embroidered the tablecloth herself, and
crocheted the head-rests on the chair.

In the evenings her cousins hung garlands of
flowers in the room, and they were strewn over

the bed and the room was sweet with their heavy fragrance.

Bano did not leave the room the day of Arshad's return. She felt weak and unable to face the women who crowded the rooms and courtyards. At the thought of food her stomach turned sour. She locked the door of her room, and would not open it until her mother-in-law made her do so in the afternoon, and forced her to drink some tea.

As she lay alone, with the sounds of the shouting chattering women shrilly penetrating the walls and locked door, she felt the intense longing for the moment of Arshad's arrival turn into a hysterical panic that exhausted her until she was drawn further and further away from herself and her surroundings and was in a void.

She woke to the sound of her name being called as impatient fists beat the door. It was dark in the room, and as she opened the door the light from the lamps outside made her draw back with hurt, dilated pupils.

She did not need to hear her cousin's words, or see her face; she did not need to feel the excitement that sent the women crowding towards the outer door. He had come home.

She shut the door, and held her hand to her heart to press back the pain. Then, because she knew he would come to her last of all, after being released from everyone's curiosity, and the clinging hungry love of the mother and the father, she tried to fill the great space between each moment with commonplace action.

She opened the door to bring in the lit gas lamp that had been put outside the room by her cousin, and by its light put fresh coals on the brazier in the corner, saw that the small night lamp had oil in it, and put it with a box of matches on the table by the vase.

The noise of excited voices made her restless. She walked to the door and back, sat on the chair, then picked up a mirror from the shelf in the wall, where she had arranged the things she needed for her toilet.

She looked at herself critically, then impatiently put the mirror down, and went to wash her face.

She dressed slowly, oiled and combed her hair, and carefully plaited it. All the women admired her thick and long plait.

Once again she picked up the mirror, outlined her eyes carefully with 'kajal', drawing out their length with steady fingers, then hesitated, powdered her face, looked again in the mirror, and with panic decision put rouge on her cheeks, and painted her lips. Then she sat on the edge of the chair and waited.

After a time she shivered, and the fire from the brazier seemed to contain no warmth. She put on her new coat, though she did not like it hiding her new sari.

There was a sound of singing outside. Someone knocked on the door but she did not open it. She got up, walked to the bed and sat on it, then back again she went to the chair. She thought she was used to waiting, but knew now she was mistaken.

"Open the door," called her cousin. "I've brought you your dinner."

"I'm not hungry," she replied.

"Not hungry? How can you be?" and the laughter was to her as the sound of frost cracking on the pond in the garden.

She set her time now by the hour for dinner. How could she have expected him earlier? He could not come until after they had eaten, and were ready to retire. Would his mother and father ever feel the need of rest tonight, and know that time was dragging, and she was waiting? Nine years of waiting closed in upon her.

It was her heart and not the door against which the hesitant hand was knocking. She picked up the mirror for a brief glance at her face, and found it saddening. She opened the door.

His unfamiliar tall silhouette and the strange smell of him drew her fears forward from the crowd of her feelings, and she stepped back in silence, her eyes downcast after the first quick, searching look.

He walked awkwardly into the room, carrying a fibre suitcase which he put down as he shut the door.

73

The gas lamp hissed to bright light in the silence; then he started, "How are . . ." cleared his throat, "How are you?"

Her ears were holding the sound of this man's voice, trying to catch in it the familiar youthful notes she had heard nine years ago; then the strong weight of her upbringing levelled all her reactions to acceptance of this stranger who was her husband.

He took advantage of her lowered eyes to look at her. The red net sari with its golden flowers spread stiffly out from below the coat tight-buttoned across her chest and hips, its belt measuring her thickened waist. The powder was too light on her skin, the rouge too pink, and the mouth held tight in shyness smudged red by in-expert hands. She looked up and away, and her eyes were large, soft and timid supplicants.

His voice strained to hide his discomfort: "I have brought a few things for you. I hope you like them." He fumbled with the locks of the suitcase. "I did not know what you would like and it was not the best time to buy anything. Would you like to take them out now?"

She slipped swiftly to her knees by the case, and with a child's eagerness began to unpack it, exclaiming with shy joy as she unwrapped each package. The two handbags and sewing-box she put aside after briefly examining them, but the gold watch she strapped on her wrist, and wore

74

the necklace and earrings of cultured pearls more proudly than if they had been real.

Then she unfolded the coat that lay beneath the sheets of tissue paper.

She liked its bright colour, and the softness of the cloth.

"I wish I could have brought something better, but it was not possible. Why don't you put it on?"

She took off her coat and threw it across the back of the armchair in her eagerness to wear the one he had brought her.

"These loose coats look better with saris," he said. He was trying to hide his uneasiness, talking to her as to a friend met after years.

She stood before him wearing his presents and her happiness as charms that lit her eyes and brought out the sweetness of her face through its masking paint.

"Thank you," she said, "thank you"—in English, though he had not spoken one word of it.

He felt a tender pity, which covered him and drove him to helpless anger against himself, his homecoming, his father, his mother, everyone.

"I must go now, Bano, to my room. I am tired."

"Go? To your room?" Incredulous surprise forced the words from her; then her hurt was submerged in the shame of what people would say when they knew. Because she could not face her thoughts, she felt her mind paralysed.

75

He could not look at her eyes, which were alive and wounded; and he spoke quickly because he hated his words.

"I cannot stay, Bano. Please try to understand. It is not because I dislike you, but because I respect you. And there is no other woman, I swear. But we are like strangers. It's not your fault, it's all my fault. I'll do anything you wish me to do—it's better that I should tell you now than later. I kept putting off writing, because I couldn't explain in a letter, and indecision makes time pass quickly. I know how I've wronged you, but what can I do now?"

His voice faded, because it did not sound convincing any more. He felt his words fall into bottomless space, not of her silence but of her incomprehension. They went to her empty of meaning, the language of a strange world, though the sounds were from hers.

The lamp hissed and shed its bright light, and around and within her was dead darkness.

He could not defend himself against this silence, and turned to go. In his clumsy haste he knocked against the small table and the unlit night lamp fell on her coat, leaving an oily trail as it rolled on to the floor.

He cursed savagely then. "I'm sorry," he said, "I am a clumsy fool."

She did not move nor speak, and because he wanted to forget his words that had struck her to

76

crumpled stillness he said with irrelevant banter, "I didn't want you to wear this old coat anyway. It reminds me of . . . my landlady . . . no, of . . . Mrs. Ram."

At last she was able to cry.

AFTER THE STORM

THE flowers were awkwardly crowded into the small-necked bottle. Its paper label had not been successfully washed away and triumphantly survived in its scratched mutilation.

On and around the bottle there was dust. There was a film of the dust on everything. It crept up with the hot wind that found its way into the room in spite of shut doors and windows. Green paper on glass panes shut out the glare that burned away colour from earth and sky and the sensual delight of vision from the eyes.

The heavy sweet scent of the flowers reached out into the skin-drying air with a cooling touch. The flowers were white and wax-petalled among thick deep green leaves. Their buds were tight wrapped in slender pale green sepals. They were allies in the battle against the cruel summer— lying cool on hot pillows—around earthenware water pots—strung in garlands sold in scented streets by singing men—adorning women when gold and silver grew heavy with heat and sweat.

This summer the battle was lost before it began. The desolation it brought was the visible expression of desolate hearts. The tainted wind blew hot from blazing homes, and carried the dust of devastated fields, and the dead . . .

She tore me out of the shroud of my thoughts, a child small and thin with serious anxious eyes and a smile on her face, a garland in her hand. She looked at the bottle and the flowers.

"Do you like them? I put them there. This is for you too." I bent my head and she slipped the garland over with a faint smile and stepped back.

"I knew you were coming today and I cleaned your room."

"Who are you?"

"Your servant. I've been put in charge of this part of the house," she said with proud responsibility.

"What is your name?"

"Bibi."

"How long have you been here?"

"A long time. Just before I left home there was the fair at Shahji's tomb." She sounded uninterested, then said brightly: "Do you need anything? The others are all sleeping. You rest and then I shall bring you some tea. I have put cold water for your bath in the buckets."

"Weren't the buckets heavy?"

"Oh no—I always brought water from the well."

I could not tell her age. Her assured manner made me feel younger than herself. Her eyes had no memories of childhood. Her body was of a

79

child of nine or ten, but its undernourished thinness was deceptive; she could have been eleven or twelve. There was no telling of how many years of childhood life had robbed her.

She came every morning with flowers no one else cared to pick, and every evening with garlands no one else cared to thread.

"Aren't they pretty? In my home we had two big bushes near the well. I made garlands for my mother and aunt."

The nails of her peasant hands were worn with work, By now I knew her story, but knew she had to tell it herself how and when she willed.

"Had you any brothers and sisters?"

"After my sister was married she went to live far away; a whole day's journey by bullock cart. My brother was older than me. He could read and write. He was clever. You will teach me, won't you?"

She kept her clothes very clean—old discarded clothes which were cut down for her and hung loosely on her. She wore tight pyjamas that were easier to clean than loose ones, and she kept her head covered like the older women, with 'dupattas' that were made from torn cotton saris. She used to dye them herself and was fond of bright colours. Her hair was combed back smoothly from a centre part, oiled and plaited with a rag. The pigtail was short and stood out stiffly. She was not a pretty child, and one would not have noticed her. But she was now a symbol and around her hovered the ghosts of all one feared.

Sometimes she threaded buds into the pierced lobes of her ears.

"I had gold earrings," she said proudly, but with no reproach. "My mother said after the next harvest she would buy me gold bangles. When we had feasts I was sorry I had no bangles."

I had bought her glass ones.

When she brought me tea she said:

"Do you like these English cakes? My mother made such lovely halwa—you would have loved it."

"Do you remember your father?"

"He died long ago. We lived with my uncle and aunt. He kept labourers to help in the fields."

One day she suddenly put her head on my lap —"I like you. Will you always keep me with you?"

Then I asked her: "Bibi—how did you come here?"

I wanted to lay my ghosts of imagined horror, and hear her tell me what actually happened.

"The police brought me. I was at the railway station. Then they took me to a place where there were lots of women and children. I ran away from them."

"Why?"

81

"I don't know. I got up at night and ran away. Then I came here."

"Who brought you?"

"The police."

Her mind refused to fill the gap between the refugee camp and her adoption.

"What happened to your mother?"

Her voice was self-detached—a child telling a fairy story. "I don't know. I was with Chand Bibi. I had gone to visit her."

"Who was she?"

"Oh, she was brave. She had a big house where I played. She fought and fought and killed so many of them—then her arm was cut off."

"Where was your mother?"

"At home. They said the house was full of blood. They said Chand Bibi kept on fighting until her arm was cut off."

"Who said?"

"Some people—I ran into the fields and a man said 'Come this way,' and he carried me, we hid in the sugar cane—then he put me on a train, and I came here. See how long this garland is. You can put it twice round your neck."

In the bottle she had put fresh flowers.

THE DAUGHTER-IN-LAW

NASIBAN was the fourth Ayah she had interviewed that week and the first who seemed suitable. To harassed Nasima Begum, for whom all problems of life had surrendered their urgency to the search for a child's nurse, Nasiban was a supernatural visitant in spite of her commonplace face and her voice that was a rusty file sawing sound. Her references were excellent, the wages she demanded were mercifully reasonable, and the tone of her voice betrayed an anxiety which encouraged bargaining.

"Allah is my witness," she said as she squatted on the floor with her voluminous white skirt spread around her, "that I would work in no other home for such pay, but . . ."

Nasima Begum said sharply: "You must remember that food and clothes are more expensive day by day. After all, it is not twenty-five rupees alone. . . ."

Nasiban was placating: "I was not complaining, Begum Sahib, though I could still get fifty or sixty rupees with the memsahibs; but one has to consider where one lives, and their servants' quarters are not suitable for young girls"—she

83

corrected herself quickly, "old women like me."

Nasima Begum was worried. "Have you any children with you?"

Nasiban smiled. "My sons, by Allah's grace, are grown men and married. I should not be working, but I do not get on with my elder daughter-in-law, and my younger son is ill and out of work, and staying with his brother." She began to smooth out her testimonials, careful of the yellowing ones tearing at the folds, and the paper rustled under her work-roughened fingers.

"The young daughter-in-law is with her mother, and I have to pay five rupees a month for her keep. It is a lot of money, but what can I do? Where can I keep her?"

She looked up hopefully for some suggestion but Nasima Begum was carefully silent.

Nasiban said, "Look at me, naked, quite naked," and she pulled down her headcloth from her greying head to show her bare neck, and empty ears pierced right round and bent over by the constant pull of the rings that once had weighed them down and stretched the lobes. "Only this pair of silver bracelets is left," she held up her wrists, "and everything else gone, though I once had a double set of gold and silver. All sold to marry my son well enough for the neighbours not to whisper and criticise."

Nasima Begum tried to console her: "A good daughter-in-law is a comfort to old age."

Nasiban said, "One gets what is one's Kismet," and she gathered her skirt around her and stood up. "I shall go now and get my things ready. God willing, I shall be back tomorrow morning. Salaam, Begum Sahib," and the room was peacefully empty of her voice.

Nasima Begum sighed with relief; the other Ayahs had wanted nothing less than fifty rupees a month.

Nasiban surprisingly proved as good as her testimonials, usually a mere formality, and sometimes even borrowed. Her voice gained through familiarity an acceptable timbre; above all, it soothed the baby, losing its rasping edge in softly chanted folk songs and lullabies. Moreover, she got on well with the other servants; even with the mother of Nathoo, Nasima Begum's old nurse and now storekeeper, who was hard to please and dominated Sufia who helped her and dusted and cleaned Nasima Begum's rooms, and Bashiran who did the sewing and mending.

While the rest of the servants lived in the quarters built a little distance from the house, the mother of Nathoo, Bashiran and Sufia lived in a low-roofed row of one-roomed 'kothris' built on one side of the large zenana courtyard with a low dividing wall in front forming a smaller courtyard in which they rested, gossiped, and sometimes worked. Nasiban was given a room between the mother of Nathoo and Bashiran, but she slept at night in the nursery.

After only a month, Nasiban was as firmly established a part of the household as if she had been there as many years as the mother of Nathoo, which were more than anyone could remember, and in whose depths even her name was lost, so that she was still the mother of Nathoo though Nathoo had died twelve years ago.

Nasiban felt the growing security of indispensability, and when the fine feelers of small requests granted had given her assurance, she said to Nasima Begum, while the tenderness of the baby's presence was still fresh one morning:

"I have had a post-card from the mother-in-law of my son. She says she cannot keep my daughter-in-law any longer for five rupees a month, and I cannot give her more."

Nasima Begum drew her face away from the baby, and with a slight frown said, "I told you I could not pay you more, and it is barely a month since you came here."

Nasiban retreated: "Begum Sahib, Allah is my witness, I do not complain; I am happy with my baby, and this is my home. But what can I do about my daughter-in-law?"

Nasima Begum relaxed: "Tell her mother you cannot give any more money yet."

Nasiban was quick to notice the qualification:

"I shall do my best; I know that your kindness will always support me." She decided to wait for a riper moment. It came sooner than she had planned. Nasima Begum came into the room a few days later in obvious agitation.

"Nasiban, I have to go away for a few days as my sister-in-law is very ill. I am sure I can leave the baby safely with you and the mother of Nathoo."

Nasiban said in vehement protestation, "The child is my very life to me. You need have no care, Begum Sahib"; then she added cautiously, "but if you will permit me to request you . . ."

Nasima Begum looked suspiciously at her, expecting the request would be for an increase in wages, but Nasiban did not mention money.

"You know, Begum Sahib, I work day and night with no care for sleep or rest. I do not grudge it, but I am old. If I could have someone to help me, make my tea in the morning, bring me my food, press my aching body . . ."

"I cannot yet . . ." began Nasima Begum.

"Begum Sahib," she went on quickly, "I ask you only if I may bring my daughter-in-law to live with me. She can sleep in my room, and she will not eat much"; then her voice hardened, "her mother has written again that she can no longer keep her for five rupees. I must give her more or take her away."

Nasima Begum felt helplessly the success of the implied threat.

The day she left, Nasiban sent for her daughter-in-law.

Whenever they found the time to sit and gossip, the women sat in the small courtyard on low rope-strung beds or squat-legged string stools. The evening her daughter-in-law arrived Nasiban came to the courtyard earlier than usual, and announced with satisfaction:

"I've made the girl sit near the baby. She must learn to be useful, and not get into bad habits, and think she has come here to play."

"Who is there to play with her?" asked Sufia, blinking her short-sighted eyes, affected by the smallpox that had scarred and pitted her round simple face. "There are no children here." Sufia had known no childhood but of work.

"Ah yes, sister Nasiban," said Bashiran, "she is very young, your daughter-in-law. She looks barely nine or ten." She looked up from the small mirror as she finished wiping the 'kajal' that had spread around her eyes. Bashiran was very careful about her appearance, kept her hair well oiled and combed into a plait, embroidered her clothes and wore ribbon bows on her slippers.

The mother of Nathoo pushed away grey wisps of hair as she lifted her head from the peas she was shelling, and defended Nasiban. "Some girls don't show their age."

Bashiran persisted: "But look at her, flat, quite flat, with a child's body."

Nasiban cleared her throat, and her voice rasped in self-pity. "I know, sister Bashiran, I know she is much too young. I was deceived. Karima Bi, the barber's wife who made the match, told me the girl was fourteen or fifteen. That was not too young for my son who, God keep him from harm, was twenty-two or twenty-three."

Bashiran interrupted, "She is not fourteen, not even twelve."

"Let her finish what she was saying," scolded the mother of Nathoo.

"When I went to her village," Nasiban continued, turning away from Bashiran, "I thought it was the elder sister Karima Bi meant me to see. I left all the arrangements to her, and she deceived me, may Allah punish her."

The mother of Nathoo nodded her head wisely: "The world has changed much since the old days."

"What was I to do?" continued Nasiban. "What can I do? The marriage cost so much money, all my savings, and I had to sell even my jewellery. I cannot afford to let my son divorce her and marry again. So I must wait until she is older before I send her to him."

"Ah well," soothed the mother of Nathoo, "she can serve you well enough meanwhile."

"But," said the persistent Bashiran, "why did her mother not keep her? You gave her five rupees a month, after all."

Nasiban was angry: "I cannot go on paying so much money, and I need someone to make my tea, press my legs, help me with the washing."

The mother of Nathoo nodded her head in approval, but Bashiran looked unconvinced and Nasiban wanted to voice her anger more, but the sound of the baby's waking cry took her away in shuffling haste.

The next three days Nasiban had little time for gossip as the baby was restless with a chill on the stomach, and during free moments she snatched sleep missed in disturbed nights. Her daughter-in-law worked to her orders, and for the rest of the time sat alone in her room, or stood silently staring at the women when they sat in the court-yard, or wandered round the inner garden plucking leaves aimlessly from the jasmine bushes. The women attempted to satisfy their curiosity by asking her questions, but after a few unsuccessful attempts to draw her out of her silence they ignored her.

Nasiban's irritability, because she could not rest enough, found release in scolding the girl at the faults she found in her at every opportunity. When the mother of Nathoo complained one evening, "Sister Nasiban, the girl does not wash your plates or her own, and heaps them on the kitchen floor. Who is to wash them?", Nasiban screamed at her daughter-in-law:

"You ill-fated one, do you think you have ser-

vants to work for you? Sister," she turned to the
mother of Nathoo, "do not spare her if she does
it again. No wonder that mother of hers deceived
me, passing her lazy good-for-nothing burden on
to me. Remember this," she scowled at her
daughter-in-law, "I will not waste words on you,
I shall have my slipper handy."

The mother of Nathoo was shaking out the
light quilt she had been sewing in preparation for
approaching cold nights. She said, "You must
accept your Kismet. She is young and will
learn."

Bashiran folded Nasima Begum's sari on which
she had been sewing a border, and putting the
thread, needle and scissors into the sewing-basket
said, "Young girls should be taught by their
mothers."

Nasiban flared: "I do not know about what
should be, but what is. I spent too much money
on her to send her back and get another one
better trained. And what more can her mother do
for her than I do?"

Her daughter-in-law sat on the bed in her
shadowed room, silently staring at the women.

Next morning Bashiran brought out her sewing-
basket, and squatting on the rug she had spread
in the verandah stretched out before her the red
silk from which she had to cut a pair of pyjamas.
She opened her basket and confidently reached
for the scissors she had put there, and not finding

them though she rummaged the contents, she emptied the basket in confusion around her.

"Aré, Sufia," she called, seeing Sufia dusting inside the room, "have you seen my scissors anywhere?"

"No, sister Nasiban." Sufia came heavy-footed to the door. "Have you lost them?"

"They are not in my basket," Bashiran said impatiently.

"Perhaps you left them in your room."

"I put them in the basket last evening," and Bashiran, after a last despairing search in the folds of the silk and under the rug, went grumbling to her room.

The mother of Nathoo was helping the cook when Bashiran called out to her, "Sister, have you seen my scissors?"

"No, what scissors?" The mother of Nathoo looked up, screwing her eyes against the stinging smoke.

"The new ones, the Angrézi ones. I've looked everywhere," said Bashiran mournfully. "And my work must be done before Begum Sahib returns."

"Perhaps Nasiban took them," and the mother of Nathoo returned to stirring the large dish of lentils, while the cook rolled the flour into fragile round 'chapātis'.

Bashiran went across the courtyard to the nursery, holding her pyjamas up from the dusty ground.

"Sister Nasiban," she said with agitated anxiety, "have you seen my scissors anywhere?"

Nasiban was folding the baby's napkins as her daughter-in-law brought them from the line.

"What scissors? I have seen none."

Bashiran sat in despair on the floor. "They are Begum Sahib's new Angrézi ones." She turned to Nasiban's daughter-in-law.

"Have you seen them?" The girl did not stop her work and silently shook her head.

Nasiban said, "She has been helping me all morning."

"Well," said Bashiran sarcastically, "jinns and ghosts must have taken them. This kind of thing never happened before. A small thing disappears, then a bigger one and a bigger one, and the next thing you know is the police are in the house."

"Really, sister Bashiran," said Nasiban, holding a half-folded napkin in her hand. "What are you hinting? We are the only newcomers in this house and jinns and ghosts don't steal scissors suddenly."

Bashiran said, "Can't open one's mouth without a strange meaning being put to one's words. Did I accuse you? If it is a crime to ask a simple question I'd better go away," and she walked away not heeding Nasiban's protests.

Nasiban stared after her: "Allah, what a temper!" and to her daughter-in-law she said, "Go, bring me some tea."

When Bashiran had finished her afternoon meal she went to the verandah to put away her sewing-things, being too depressed to work. As she picked up the silk the scissors clattered to the floor, startling her.

"Hai! hai!" she shouted, and picking them up, she went back to where the others were still eating. She brandished the scissors and said in puzzled and shamed anger: "Look at them. There they were, lying under the silk. I shook that very piece of silk out. You saw me, didn't you, Sufia?"

"So I did," said Sufia, her eyes round with surprise.

The mother of Nathoo said, as she mixed the rice and vegetables with her fingers, "It is easy to make a mistake sometimes."

"It was not a mistake," said Bashiran angrily, and seeing Nasiban's daughter-in-law sitting on the steps of her room eating silently from the tin-plate in her lap, she thought of Nasiban, and her anger increased.

The next afternoon, both Nasiban and Bashiran had put aside thoughts of the previous evening's bickering unpleasantness. They were sitting on the verandah, and Bashiran was sewing a piece of lace on the baby's frock for Nasiban, when the mother of Nathoo came shuffling across the court-yard in agitation.

"I can't find my keys, I've looked everywhere. Have you seen them anywhere?"

"I have not been away from the nursery," said Nasiban.

"I have been working here," said Bashiran.

"Sufia says she knows nothing," said the mother of Nathoo.

"And my daughter-in-law has been with me."

"I put them under my pillow when I rested, as I always do, and I was away only for a few minutes, but when I looked for them they had gone."

"Just like my scissors," said Bashiran.

"You found them after all," reminded Nasiban, and they looked at each other with a reviving flicker of resentment.

The mother of Nathoo wailed: "I have to take out the tea and sugar. What am I to do?"

"Just like my scissors," repeated Bashiran smugly.

"I've looked properly, I tell you. I do not make a fuss without being sure."

"What do you mean?" Bashiran flared. "I made no needless fuss—Sufia knows . . ." Before she could finish Sufia appeared saying, "Sister, here are your keys. I found them by your doorstep."

The mother of Nathoo said as Bashiran had done, "But I had searched everywhere. Allah knows, I am not blind."

"My scissors . . ." began Bashiran, but the mother of Nathoo glared and walked away loudly.

Nasiban said, "How strange this is," and Bashiran replied, "Just as if there were jinns in the house." Sufia cried out in superstitious fear, "God forbid."

Nasiban's daughter-in-law walked from the courtyard to the nursery without looking at the women.

The very next morning Nasiban's voice raised in anger preceded her into the courtyard. She came in with her skirt whirling around her, holding up a baby frock from which hung torn lace that had been wrenched off, tearing the silk.

"Look at this," she shouted. "Just look at it."

Bashiran and Sufia were dyeing muslin 'dupattas', and their hands were stained red with the dye. The mother of Nathoo was sitting on the steps cleaning grains of rice in a large plate. They looked up at Nasiban in surprise, and Bashiran said sarcastically, "Is this the work of jinns?"

"Whose is it?" said Nasiban, looking angrily around.

The mother of Nathoo, smarting with yesterday's memories, said coldly, "Who can tell?"

"Whoever it is," said Nasiban, "seems to pick and choose very well."

"Who," asked Sufia, sitting back on her haunches, "who are you accusing? I'm the only one the jinns have not visited."

Nasiban was taken aback by this unexpected retort from the humble Sufia. She said plaintively,

"Sister Sufia, did I say it was you? But look at this," and she held up the torn frock. "What will I say to Begum Sahib?"

The mother of Nathoo said drily: "There'll be much to tell her. A few days away from the house, and the sky seems to be falling on our heads."

Bashiran said suddenly: "The jinns have spared your daughter-in-law. Why not ask her about it?"

Nasiban flared: "Why not?"

She went into the room, and from its dark depths dragged out the girl by her thin arm, and in a voice harshly and loudly authoritative demanded, "Do you know anything about this?" and held up the frock to the girl, who drew back her head and shook it silently.

"Are you telling the truth?" She shook her.

The girl nodded.

Bashiran said, "You don't expect her to say anything else, do you?"

Nasiban replied, "What do you want me to do? Beat her?" And as she moved forward, the girl drew back flinching.

"Wait, sister," said Bashiran, "now you'll accuse me of making you beat her."

The mother of Nathoo said, "It will not help you to fight with each other."

"What will help me?" rasped Nasiban.

Sufia and Bashiran stood up, and holding by its corners the fine muslin waved it gently to dry it. Sufia hesitated, then said:

97

"Last night, I had to get up in the middle of the night, and I saw her walking up and down this courtyard laughing and talking to herself. I was so frightened that, though my stomach ached, I waited until morning."

"Ai hai," gasped Bashiran with eyes wide open.

"Really, sister," started Nasiban angrily, but the mother of Nathoo interrupted:

"Why didn't you say this before, Sufia?"

"I did not wish to say anything in case sister Nasiban thought I cast doubts on the rightness of her daughter-in-law's mind. But when strange things keep happening, and I am suspected . . ."

"Who said you were suspected?" Nasiban demanded fiercely.

"It's no use quarrelling," said the mother of Nathoo with the authority of her age. "One can never tell; sometimes the mind is sick, sometimes a jinn possesses it. One must . . ."

Nasiban, trembling with impotent rage, cried: "You talk as if you were certain she were a lunatic or possessed by a devil. Whatever it be, she is my Kismet's burden; she must stay with me. If I am not wanted here, say it clearly; tell the Begum Sahib, or better still, I'll tell her."

"Be calm," reproached the mother of Nathoo. "I meant no harm."

"Why," suggested Bashiran, "don't you ask her what she was doing last night?"

Nasiban pulled her daughter-in-law towards

her and threatened: "What were you doing at night? Tell me the truth or I shall beat you so you will remember it all your miserable life." She hated the girl in the presence of the three women's accusing curiosity.

"I was chasing the rabbits away."

"Rabbits? What rabbits?" the three women said together.

"There are no rabbits here," said the mother of Nathoo.

"Where could they come from?" said Sufia.

"She could not talk to rabbits," said Bashiran.

"Tell me the truth," said Nasiban, raising her hand.

"From that drain," pointed her daughter-in-law. "There were lots of them."

Bashiran went towards the drain, and called out: "I knew she was lying. I remember there was wire netting put across the opening when the wild cat came in. See, there it is. Rabbits, indeed!"

Nasiban turned towards her daughter-in-law and struck her sharply across the face, and then dragged her by the wrist: "Come with me, ill-fated one. Come and sit by me, and don't dare to move further than my eyes can guard you."

Sufia said softly as the three women stared after her: "She does not cry when she is beaten; they never do if they are possessed."

"Be quiet," said the mother of Nathoo.

"Rabbits!" repeated Bashiran with scorn.

It was so early the next morning when Sufia's wailing voice woke them that the dew was not dry on the leaves.

"Sister Bashiran! Oh mother of Nathoo!" And because she knew how heavy was the sleep of the mother of Nathoo, she wailed near the door of her room.

When the women came out of their dark rooms blinking at the early light, yawning and grumbling, she held before them her crumpled headcloth splashed with red as if it had staunched a gushing artery. "Look," she cried.

"Allah," gasped the mother of Nathoo, "what is this? What has happened?"

"Blood," screamed Bashiran.

"It's not blood," shouted Sufia in sobbing irritation. "It's dye, can't you see?"

The mother of Nathoo sat on the steps exhausted by relief: "I thought you had been stabbed."

Bashiran said in disappointed anger: "Wah! You wail and wake the house as if you were being murdered, and for what?"

"For what, you ask!" Sufia cried. "Look at this," and she shook the dirty piece of reddened cloth. "I'm a poor woman; I can't afford new clothes. Am I to wear this?"

Bashiran said, "It's the dye we used yesterday," and she went to the upturned bowl under which they had kept the powdered dyes in folded pieces of paper.

She called out, "The red packet is not here. I think I know where it is," and she went towards the room of Nasiban's daughter-in-law. "See, there is some of it scattered on the doorstep," and she knocked violently on the door, shouting, "Open the door! Open the door! She shuts the door and sleeps, and does not die in the heat inside, the devil."

There was no sound.

The mother of Nathoo said: "This cannot go on. Your scissors, my keys and then this. We must find out who is doing this mischief. You had better ask Nasiban to come here. Sister Bashiran, wait for her."

Sufia went to call Nasiban, and Bashiran went to her room to put her slippers on before going to the tap to rinse her dry mouth. She stumbled out as if pushed out, her voice shrill and cracking. "Allah's curse on the wretch! Look, sister," and she thrust under the very nose of the mother of Nathoo her slippers with their ribbon bows wrenched off and dipped in red dye.

She hammered with her slippers on the door of Nasiban's daughter-in-law. "Come out, you devil, come out."

The mother of Nathoo calmed her: "Wait for Nasiban," but with a feeling of disquiet she went into her room to see if she had been spared. Everything seemed in order except that the quilt she had kept on the wooden box in the corner after sunning it seemed, now that she looked so carefully, to be folded differently. She took it up and shook it. "Allah!" she screamed in horror, and tears burned her eyes. The green silk she had so carefully quilted was smeared with streaks and daubs of red. "Hai, Allah," she cried, "it is ruined, the beautiful silk Begum Sahib gave me."

Bashiran forgot her own sorrow for the moment, it seemed to her much less by contrast. "Sister," she said mournfully, "it is indeed ruined. That stain will not come off."

"I can't get another; I can't sew it all over again," wailed the mother of Nathoo. Then her mounting anger dried her tears and she went out and cursed by the locked door.

"If you did this, you wretch, I'll kill you, mother-in-law or no mother-in-law."

"What is the matter? What is the matter?" called out Nasiban as she came into the courtyard, and there was a preparatory edge of aggression in her voice. "I have hardly time to give baby his feed, and there stands sister Sufia saying over and over again 'Come with me' and no more, though I say to her, 'What is it, in Allah's name, what is it?'"

"What is it?" screamed the mother of Nathoo, pushing back strands of her hair from her distraught face. "This is it," and she shook the quilt before her while Bashiran thrust forward the slippers.

"And this."

"And this," said Sufia, picking up the stained headcloth from the ground where she had thrown it in disgust.

"But, mother of Nathoo, sister . . ." started Nasiban, perplexed.

"And now will you ask that devil to come out?" said the mother of Nathoo, pointing to the locked door.

Bashiran and Sufia added their loud accusations, and the weight of the noise crushed Nasiban. She pleaded, "Be patient," then knocked on the door, rattling its heavy chain.

"Come out of there; are you deaf or dead?"

The door opened, and her daughter-in-law stood clinging to it, the whites of her eyes startling against her dark skin as she looked at each woman without turning her head.

"Why did you not open the door?"

There was no reply.

"Did you do this mischief?" Nasiban's voice rose to the point of cracking as she held up the quilt and 'dupatta'.

The girl shook her head.

"The liar, the unholy liar," the women screamed around her. Bashiran pulled the girl's hands from under the 'dupatta' which covered them. "Look," she said triumphantly, pointing at the reddened fingers, the dye-encrusted nails. "She didn't know it does not wash off easily."

"The wretch, the ungrateful wretch." The mother of Nathoo shook with anger.

"She is mad," said Sufia.

Nasiban's face was drawn with rage and shame: "You ill-begotten, ill-fated wretch. What can I do to you?" And in a frenzy she beat the girl.

Sufia said, "See, she does not cry. She has a devil in her."

The mother of Nathoo said bitterly, "She has no devil—she is wicked."

Nasiban turned away, worn out by her emotions. "And if she is mad or wicked or possessed, what am I to do? I've asked you over and over again."

"Return her to her mother," said Bashiran.

"I cannot, and you know it," snapped Nasiban.

"She cannot stay here," said the mother of Nathoo. "She is so wicked she will even kill someone some day."

"If she cannot stay, I cannot stay," said Nasiban.

"If she stays, I will not," said the mother of Nathoo, glaring at Nasiban.

Bashiran and Sufia stared in surprise. The mother of Nathoo could no more leave than the house move itself from its foundations.

Bashiran said to pacify them: "Wait until

Begum Sahib returns. She will decide what is to be done."

The girl stood silently against the door. Nasiban turned and scowled: "Come with me, you devil. I'll not leave you a moment alone, and at night I'll lock you in."

The unpleasantness in the courtyard had started like the small circling eddies of air that sometimes danced around it catching in a whirl dust and fallen leaves, before fading away ghost-like as the scattered dust and leaves settled into stillness, but it grew steadily in its circular reach and violence, until now it spread beyond the courtyard and enclosed the whole house; and at its centre was the daughter-in-law, once a shadow and now being invested with a dark reality.

The woman who swept the compound and cleaned the bathrooms heard from Sufia of the misdeeds of Nasiban's daughter-in-law. She told the washerman's wife, the gardeners' wives and the watchman's wife when she went to the servants' quarters. The cook and his helper in the kitchen were told of the cause of the mother of Nathoo's ill humour, and told the bearer who served at the table. He told the man who helped him, who told the man who dusted the outer rooms, who told the watchman, who told the chauffeur.

Everyone found excuses to come inside to see the daughter-in-law of Nasiban who was mad or possessed of a devil. They were ready with suggestions to cure her and cast out the spirit.

Nasiban scowled and grumbled at everyone, and her daughter-in-law sat by her impassively staring at those who stared at her.

Into this unquiet atmosphere returned Nasima Begum. She went straight to the nursery, and the fulfilment of her impatient joy enclosed her as she held her baby in her arms; but Nasiban's mournful self-pity pierced through and she asked with anxious surprise:

"What is the matter, Nasiban? Why do you look so sad? Is anything wrong? Baby looks well enough, thank God."

"Ah yes," sighed Nasiban heavily, "may the evil eye be far from him. Allah has rewarded the care I have taken, putting my very life into my work, not knowing whether it was day or night."

"What is it then?" said Nasima Begum impatiently.

"Ask the mother of Nathoo, ask Bashiran, ask Sufia, ask the household. I'll say nothing." Nasiban's voice was a martyr's.

Nasima Begum's anger swelled in proportion to her impaired happiness. "What is the meaning of all this? Go then and call the mother of Nathoo."

There was no need to do so. The mother of Nathoo, frowning, holding up her trailing pyjamas, was already stumbling impatiently towards the verandah, followed by Bashiran and Sufia.

"Salaam, Begum Sahib," she said, her breath rapid with effort and impatience as she painfully climbed the steps. Her complaining voice drowned the "Salaams" of Bashiran and Sufia, who followed her.

"Allah be thanked you have come back. The things that have been happening in this house since you went away!"

"Salaam, mother of Nathoo, but will you, for heaven's sake, tell me what the matter is? I cannot understand why Nasiban refuses to say anything, and stands there weeping."

Nasiban's voice quavered with self-pity. "Who will believe me, a mere newcomer?"

"Wah, sister," flamed the mother of Nathoo, and Bashiran and Sufia were her chorus.

In the released deluge of words, gesticulations, accusations, threats, appeals to Allah and cries to heaven, there kept appearing, disappearing and appearing again "the daughter-in-law of Nasiban."

"If that daughter-in-law of Nasiban's lives here, I refuse to stay," declared the mother of Nathoo.

Nasiban said acidly, "Why should you go? I shall leave."

Nasima Begum's patience was worn by weariness, and distaste of the quarrelling women.

"Be quiet," she ordered, and surprised them into silence.

"Nasiban, bring your daughter-in-law here."

Nasiban came back in a short while, pulling the reluctant girl by her arm: "Here is the ill-fated wretch."

Nasima Begum looked up and exclaimed with shocked surprise: "Why! It's a child."

"Not a child, a she-devil," said the mother of Nathoo.

"Possessed by a devil," corrected Sufia.

"A wicked, wretched child," said Bashiran.

"A child, yes, a child. I was cheated," said Nasiban.

Nasima Begum looked into the frightened animal eyes of the shrinking child, and her heart was tight with pity.

"Come here, child, what is your name?" The women scowled at the softness of her voice.

"Munni," whispered the girl, distrustful of the unexpected kindness.

"Why did you do these things, Munni?" Nasima Begum asked gently.

"I don't remember doing anything," the girl said.

"Aré, the liar," said Bashiran.

"She's cunning," said the mother of Nathoo.

Sufia said nothing.

"Do with her what you will, she's my Kismet's curse," said Nasiban.

The girl shrank back, and her mouth grew sullen.

"But, Munni," said Nasima Begum persuasively, "look at your hands. They are still red."

The girl put her small red hands behind her back, and stared silently, the whites of her eyes again startling.

Nasima Begum sighed and said: "Will you all go now. I am tired. Nasiban, wait a moment. Why don't you send her home to her mother?"

Nasiban protested: "Her mother says she is married and not her responsibility."

"But she's a child," Nasima Begum reproached her.

"I was cheated, Begum Sahib," and Nasiban repeated her story of the marriage, adding obstinately, "I've spent too much money getting my son married. I cannot find him another wife." Then she added with an angry look at her daughter-in-law: "I'll teach her. She's not been beaten enough."

"No," said Nasima Begum sharply. "Don't beat her."

Munni looked up in surprise.

Nasiban was quick to sense her advantage. "Perhaps I could persuade her mother to take back the girl if I promised to pay more. But I can't afford it on my pay."

Nasima Begum said impatiently, "Go now. I'll

think about it. Munni, be a good girl, go and help
your mother-in-law," and she touched the girl
lightly on the head. Munni's eyes were a tamed
animal's.

That night Nasiban locked her daughter-in-
law again in her room. In the middle of the night
Bashiran was wakened by screams, and incessant
banging of the locked door next to hers. At last,
unable to sleep, though she tried to ignore the
noise, she opened the door and stepped outside.
Sufia, who had also heard the noise, joined her.

Bashiran shouted through the door: "Be quiet,
wretched girl. Do you want to wake the entire
household? Be quiet."

"Let me out. Open the door," screamed the
girl.

"Hai," grumbled Bashiran. "She'll wake the
dead, but the mother of Nathoo still snores."

She unlatched the door, and the silence was
sudden and deep. The girl stood against the wall,
a trembling faint shape.

"What do you want?" said Bashiran harshly.

"Keep the door open. They can't get out," the
girl said, her voice hoarse with screaming and
crying.

"Who can't get out? She's pretending again,
seeing rabbits, I suppose. Go to sleep. You slept
last night well enough, but now you want Begum
Sahib to hear you and be sorry for you. You're a
cunning one."

"Go to sleep," said Sufia gently, because she was frightened.

As Bashiran moved to close the door the girl screamed and pushed the door open. "No . . . no . . . no."

"Be quiet."

"Sister Bashiran," said Sufia, "there is nothing we can do. Shall I wake the mother of Nathoo?"

"She will sleep even if the sky falls on her, and that wretched Nasiban is safe in the nursery. Leave the door open, and let her murder everyone. I shall lock myself in."

They left the sobbing girl in the darkness and the silence.

In the morning when Nasima Begum woke for the morning prayers, she saw through the wire mesh of the door the huddled form of the girl. After the first sick moment of surprised fright she opened the door. The girl was curled up and covered completely by her 'dupatta' against the fresh chill of early morning. Nasima Begum shook her gently.

"Munni, Munni."

The girl started up in surprise, her eyes again a frightened animal's until recognition absorbed terror.

"Munni, what are you doing here?"

"I was frightened in my room."

"Come in here." Nasima Begum switched on the light.

"What frightened you?"

"The same thing."

"What thing?"

"The big black man with a tiger's face. Sometimes it's a dog's face. And he puts his knee on my chest, and then I can't breathe. And the rabbits run round the room, and then he says something to me, and I don't know what it is."

The girl was talking mechanically with no expression.

"But, Munni, you must be dreaming. There can't be such things, or other people would see them."

"Oh, but they are there, almost every night since that night."

"Which night."

"My mother said to my sister 'Go and bring wood.' My sister said I had to go with her and she went to the mango grove. I said 'Don't go there, it's a dark place,' but she pulled my ears and I said 'There's a grave there,' but she took me. Then she said 'Climb that tree,' and when I did she ran away, and I jumped and fell over the grave, and a man ran after me up to the village. My mother was angry because we brought no wood."

"Did you tell her what happened?"

"Yes, I did. I had fever all night, but my sister said I was lying and no one ran after me, and she said ghosts were in peepul trees, not mango trees."

"But, Munni, they are nowhere."

"Oh yes they are. What about the woman who sat near the well, and sang all the time? Everybody was kind to her because they knew she was possessed by one. They specially like you if you wear jewellery and dress up, everyone knows that. The woman got like that when she was dressed up for a wedding."

"And were you dressed up?"

The girl nodded shyly.

"Oh I see, it was after you were married."

"I had on a red dupatta. They like red."

"Who told you all these things, Munni?"

"Oh, I heard," she said vaguely.

"But, Munni, don't you know if there are devils and ghosts they don't come near when you take God's name. Did your mother teach you any prayers?"

"No," said the girl.

"Did you tell her about the things you see?"

"No."

"Why?"

"They didn't come so often, and didn't stay so long, and she would not have believed me because my sister said I pretended."

"Listen to me, Munni. I'll teach you something. You say it every night when you go to bed and nothing wicked will come near you. Now repeat after me . . ."

Nasima Begum said each word carefully, and

the girl's faltering tongue fumbled as she repeated the simple prayer.

Nasiban's harsh voice broke the unreal bond between them.

"Salaam, Begum Sahib, I came because I heard her voice. What mischief are you up to now?"

"None," said Nasima Begum shortly. "I wanted to talk to her."

"Salaam, Begum Sahib," came Bashiran's voice from the door. "Here she is! I was frightened to think where she could have gone, what she could have done. If she is to murder our nights as she did last night, we will need to be angels to work the next day. Begum Sahib, how long must we endure this?"

"Decide what you wish, Begum Sahib," Nasiban interrupted. "But if I go away and take her with me, this trouble and bickering will end. It is my Kismet that I must be separated from my baby just when he has got to know me well and love me, but what can I do?" She turned to the girl, "Come, unfortunate one," and she went out of the room followed by the reluctant girl.

Nasima Begum sighed: "This is an auspicious way to start the day. Stop your grumbling, Bashiran."

As the sun swung into greater clarity of heat, and the dim shapes of morning lost their intangibility, from Nasima Begum's mind there began to fade the fantastic impressions of her strange conversation with Munni.

Nasiban's whimpering self-pity, Bashiran's monotonous grumbling, the sullenness of the mother of Nathoo, the stupid gloom of Sufia, the baby's attachment to Nasiban, were, by contrast, sharply real. Also the fact that the cause of all the unpleasantness was the daughter-in-law of Nasiban.

"Poor little thing," sighed Nasima Begum, and her pity was by now sifted into an abstraction.

She decided to buy peace.

When Nasiban was taking her daughter-in-law back to her mother now that her pay was increased and she could pay eight rupees a month, the women were sitting in the courtyard.

"See that she takes nothing with her," said Bashiran, "except her devil."

"Let her take anything as long as she takes herself," said the mother of Nathoo.

"Take her to the tomb of the Saint," advised Sufia.

Nasiban said to her daughter-in-law, not replying directly to the women:

"Open your box, unroll your bedding and let them see what you have inside. Let this be my last share of shame."

Her daughter-in-law went into the room, and as Nasiban followed she whispered, her eyes tormented and pleading:

"Let me stay and work for Begum Sahib. I'll be good, I swear it."

Nasiban said impatiently, "Hurry, I have no time to waste."

That night when Nasima Begum went to her room she found, on her dressing-table, the frame twisted and the glass broken of the group of her husband, her baby and herself. Her photograph had been torn out.

THE LOSS

SHE shook me awake. My mind was shocked into a blank whiteness by the violence of its uprooting from dark depths. I saw with un-recognising terror the ugliness of the face sus-pended above me, its misshapen quivering mouth, its tortured eyes. I stared in rigid fear at the night-mare face until fugitive consciousness crept back transforming it. In the face, familiar to my mind and heart, of the woman whose heavy breasts had nourished me, whose rough hands had tended me, there was no ugliness. "My child, my child," she cried. "Wake up. Help me. I am lost. I am lost." Fear returned easily in the sadness of the silence before dawn. "What is it? Has anything happened to Chand?" "No, no, God forbid, God strike his enemies," she prayed in superstitious terror for her son, then wailed, "I am the accursed of Fate. I am lost. I have been robbed." "Robbed?" My incredulity was born of years of security. She nodded her head, choking as she wiped her streaming eyes and nose with her white headcloth.

I put my arm round her shaking, shapeless body: "The children will wake up. Come with me to your room and tell me what has happened."

She followed me down the dim corridor slowly. Her cracked bare feet were always swollen and could not easily carry her heavy body. I opened the door to the terrace, to the growing light, and she painfully walked down the stone steps to the inner courtyard where the maidservants lived. I felt a sudden tender consciousness of her age.

Her crying grew louder, and by the time we were outside her room she was unrestrained in the expression of her despair. She sat on the stone steps and swayed, chanting:

"My Kismet, my Kismet, I am accursed."

I shook her and said sharply, "Tell me, for God's sake, what has happened."

"From under my bed," she said thickly, "he took it from under my bed. I must have been dead, not asleep."

"What was it?"

She stared blankly and said slowly: "Perhaps it was not there when I went to sleep. I didn't look, I was so tired, so tired."

I remembered the gaiety of the party that night, the many guests, the quantity and variety of food she had helped to prepare. "What are you talking about?"

"My box, my steel box. Everything I had in the world was in it." The women servants were crowding into the courtyard, wakened by the lamentations, and drawn by their curiosity. My presence silenced their staring sympathy.

I had to bend my head to pass through the low door into the tiny room lighted dimly by a small, barred window. In that confined space her bundled possessions crowded into anonymity. The low bed, its string centre sagging, was pulled up on its side against the wall, its meagre bedding wrapped in a worn mat balanced across the rough wooden frame and leg. She had pushed it aside as an obstacle to her searching incredulous eyes, which still strove to conjure back the box into the empty space that held its traces on the mud floor. It must have been quite a small box.

Beyond the bed a door led into a dark storeroom, its air heavily stale, with a heavy wooden door opening towards the garden. The locks on both doors were broken. I went back to the courtyard and said nothing was to be moved or touched.

She looked at me as one who begs for a miracle, believing in spite of everything. "Help me, my child, help me." The thin grey hair of her uncovered head was disordered. Her grief obsessed me, who remembered the warm shelter of her love in all childhood's sorrows.

Some of the menservants had by now joined the women in the courtyard. They were chattering in confusion, each trying to clear suspicion with expressions of sorrow or anger, with suggestions, explanations, alibis.

"Help me, pity me."

At the sound of her voice my eyes burned. I turned on the others in a rage. "What are you staring at? Stop your empty chatter. Have you no work to do? Go, get out of here."

Surprised and afraid they began to leave.

I caressed her grey head: "What was in the box? Tell me."

"Everything I have saved, every pice. All my jewellery, too, and the gold I had put aside for Chand's wife when he marries." It was hard to understand her words spaced between sobs. "Now he will have nothing, he will appear a beggar."

I said in stupid despair: "Why did you put it in a box and under your bed? I thought you had listened to me and Chand, and had put it in the bank."

"They told me there was fighting and trouble, and the banks were not safe." It was a simple peasant woman speaking. I said bitterly:

"You might as well have buried it."

"Where could I have done so?" Her simplicity shamed me.

"Why did you not tell me?"

"I was afraid you would be angry." She cried like a child.

"When did Chand take it out of the bank?"

"A month ago."

"Did anyone else know about the box?"

"I do not know. I cannot remember what may have been said."

Wearily I said, "I had better send for Chand, and telephone the police." She implored me:

"They will take no notice of a poor woman's loss, ask the Deputy Sahib himself. If you ask him he will surely help. Don't ask the men at the police station, I pray you." The pattern of her invocation was familiar. Even God she approached through a hierarchy of saints.

I left her sitting on the steps. Freed from the encompassing presence of her grief it seemed exaggerated. I felt the irritation of the discomforting formalities of a police investigation, and the disturbing, threatening presence of a thief in the house.

It seemed a long time before Chand came. He looked distressed and kept his eyes lowered. His usual familiarity which stung me with its arrogant veil of respect was absent. He walked behind me towards his mother's room. In childhood he had dominated me, beaten me in every game, being stronger and more decisive. His mother had always made the balance even between us, scolding and beating him when I ran to her in tears. It was because she loved him and wished him to learn his position early in life. He could not understand then, and neither did I. As we grew older I saw less of him. His mother brought him to me whenever he was in trouble because she was confident I would not fail her. Besides, he was my foster-brother. I stopped suddenly and said: "You should have told me about the bank."

"She told me not to."

"You should have known better than to allow her to keep money and jewels in a box under her bed."

"I did not know. I did not know about the box. I thought she had hidden everything in one of the store-rooms. She has the keys after all."

I felt surprised; I had taken it for granted that she had no secrets from him.

"Do you know what has been stolen?"

He said in a distressed voice: "Everything. There were four hundred rupees in cash, three thousand rupees worth of gold and jewellery, and some pieces of silk. She said it was all being saved for me."

"Three thousand!" I calculated instinctively that the present value was more than four times as much.

With over twelve thousand she could have considered herself a woman of means. Yet she worked for ten rupees a month, and had started thirty years ago on eight. I saw her poverty and self-denial with intense clarity in the light of her lost savings. I walked on slowly: "There will be a lot to do when the police come. I want you to tell the servants they must be ready for questioning."

She was still sitting on the steps. She had not

washed, nor eaten, and when she saw us, she began to cry again.

"Hush, Amma," Chand said, and there were tears in his eyes.

She said in a loud high-pitched wail : "I am destitute, a beggar. I am at the mercy of the lowest. What am I now that I should live?"

I looked at her in bewilderment. "What am I now?" What she had been yesterday, and the day before, and the day before through the accepted years.

She had come from her village when I was born, the simple daughter of poor farmers who had once owned land themselves. She never forgot that, and the earthborn pride withstood extremes of poverty. She had lost her husband when her child was born, and when her mother-in-law said the child was accursed, and had brought misfortune to the house, her love for it became a protective passion. She was considered favoured by Kismet that the estate manager had found her in his search for a foster-mother for the landlord's eldest child.

She was examined by doctors, and they tested her blood and milk. She submitted to every trial because she wanted an asylum for her child.

He was taken from her breast and fed on cow's milk so that she should nurse me, and a special maidservant looked after him so that she should devote all her time to me. She was paid eight rupees a month, given three sets of clothes that she should always be clean, special food that her milk should be rich, and on feast days and birthdays she was given presents of money, clothes or gold jewellery. Her child wore my old clothes. She hoarded everything for the day her son would marry and bring home his bride to care for her in her old age.

When I grew too old for her constant care she was put in charge of the stores and kitchen. It was responsible and hard work in a household where the smallest number of people to be fed was twenty, as most of the servants were given food as part of their wages.

Her work in the kitchen with its smoking logs made it hard for her to look clean any more, and her clothes looked crumpled because she wore them night and day. She changed them now like the other maidservants did, once a week when the washerman brought his weekly wash. Then she was transformed to her old self with her starched white headcloth, striped cotton shirt and dark checked pyjamas. The three silver bangles on each wrist and the silver rings on her thick fingers were worn with age, and the silver did not shine. All day she was weighing, measuring, grinding wheat, cleaning rice and lentils, curdling milk, helping the cook, making preserves, sweets, delicacies. Or she would sit in the courtyard sewing, with thick-lensed spectacles low on her nose, their broken frames held together with thick thread. She relaxed only when she lay on her string bed for a short afternoon's rest, or sat on the lawn of an evening watching the children play, or on the floor by me while I ate something she had specially cooked for me. And, of course, when Chand came to see her.

I called her Amma, and to my children she was "Granny." She was privileged to correct me, and she could scold them. Sometimes a new servant would anger her, speaking to her as to an equal. Then she grumbled and threatened to go back to her village, but no one took the threat seriously, not she herself.

I went through school and college, was married and had children. She did not change through the years. Only her hair was thinner and grey, she had lost a few of her even teeth, and walked more heavily.

And now she cried, "Who am I? I am a beggar at the mercy of the lowest," and all that had been simple, unquestioned and changeless changed. I saw it now, clearly. It had not been enough, the abstraction of love and respect; it had not made poverty and hard work bearable. The power had been in the little box under the bed. The money and gold had brought her no visible comfort, but were an assurance of it. The rich foundation was gone, and her poor life crumbled.

125

"What am I, robbed of my possessions?" her grief cried.

"What am I without mine?" my heart echoed in fearful recognition.

I said to Chand, "Try and persuade her to eat. I have work to do."

Her loss was suddenly mine. When I rang my friend I consciously subordinated his position of authority as a police officer to my friendship. I insisted that the investigation should be more than a matter of routine, that he should put his best men on the job and stop at nothing. He was surprised at my earnestness, and said he would come himself.

The two men who came with him were obviously impressed by his presence and evident interest. They went through the necessary wearisome formalities.

The servants were uneasy, some of them sullen, under the weight of suspicion.

She was calmer, strengthened by props to her hopes. She had no doubt that so much skilled effort would be successful. She had faith in me, therefore in my friend.

The days went by with no tangible result. Her fits of hysterical weeping were followed by exhausted calm. The effect on the household was disturbing, and the servants were turning from sympathy to resentment aggravated by hated police surveillance. "It was the will of God. Why

cry at Fate? While one has two hands and movement in one's limbs one can work and live."

I threatened to dismiss anyone who angered her.

She went about her work silently, not seeming
to care about the others' constraint in her presence. Chand was with her every evening when
he had finished his work in the garage where he
was a mechanic.

As the son of my foster-mother he had been
taught with me by my tutor. Later he was sent to
a municipal school but kept running away. He
said he wanted to be a mechanic and was appren-
ticed to a garage. She had hoped he would be
content to work as my personal attendant. He
liked to wear the old suits I gave him, but his
mother would not let him wear a tie in her
presence, nor smoke. "Who do you think you
are?" she said in disgust. "A rich man or a
sahib?"

He wore his hair long, well oiled and brushed
back from a side parting. In his mother's presence
he kept it covered carefully with his cloth cap
because she wanted him to crop it as simple
working men do.

She saved her meagre pay to give him money
when he asked for it. The first time I knew about
it was when I went to see her about a servant who
wished to leave because she had abused him. I
noticed her dry mouth. She was not chewing
'pān' as she constantly did. With the tobacco in it

that had blackened her teeth and lips it was a drug without which she was nervous and irritable.

I asked her, "Are you fasting that you eat no pān?"

"I have none," she said abruptly.

"Why not?"

"I have no money."

I was angry: "You could have asked me for some."

"I do not wish to trouble you with small matters."

"Your comfort is no small matter." I forced her to take the money and in giving it was ashamed that it meant so little to me and so much to her. The only luxury she allowed herself was jasmine oil for her hair. She used ground charcoal to clean her teeth, and ground gram flour instead of soap. But 'pān' was a necessity, and all the small things that went with it, lime and betel nut and tobacco.

"On what did you spend your money?"

"Everything is expensive," she said evasively.

I had to plead with her as a child asks a favour before she told me she was saving money, grudging every spent pice because Chand told her he was in debt. I made her promise then to come to me when she needed anything. "You treat me as a stranger. Am I not your child?" She was tearfully grateful, and my embarrassment turned to resentment when I thought of Chand.

I did not wish to interfere with the police, but the fruitless days seemed unending. The restive servants were by now openly contemptuous of the police. They had more faith in their own traditional methods of discovering thieves and asked me if I would help by reading some prayers. I was irritable and said they were free to be superstitious fools in their spare time, then dismissed the matter from my mind. I avoided her because her faith exposed the lie of my consolation. She seemed calmer but unnaturally quiet. One night when Chand did not come she was found by the watchman wandering on the street, a little distance from the house. She had not stepped out of the gates in thirty years on more occasions than one could remember in counting. She did not even know the name of the street. Always she went out in a curtained carriage or walked ghostlike behind her escort in her veiling 'burqa', preferably after dark. The night the watchman found her she was alone and unveiled. I went to see my friend next morning, bitter and angry at delaying inefficiency.

His answer shocked me. "We are doing our best, and from the information we have been able to gather we suspect Chand. I wish to detain him for questioning."

"Chand! You must be mad. Good God! Why should he do it? He sees her suffering. Besides, what motive could he have to take what is after all his?"

"He gambles, he has recently lost a lot, and he is keeping a woman."

"But he is a human being."

"Please don't be childish," he said cynically. "All I know is he must be properly questioned."

"What do you mean by 'properly'? You must not hurt him. It would kill her."

When we were children Chand was once caned. I ran and hid my face in her lap. At each stroke he screamed, and I felt the responsive quiver of her body, and her hot tears on my neck.

"You are being unnecessarily dramatic," he said coldly.

"If you detain him she will find out, and I am afraid for her because her mind is affected already."

"What do you expect me to do? There is no alternative but to drop the whole matter."

"Are you certain about Chand?"

"In my own mind yes, but naturally there must be proof to eliminate the small element of doubt."

"You have put a strange choice before me."

"You realise that normally you would have had no choice?"

"I appreciate that, but what am I to do now? You may be wrong and she still may get back what she has lost. But you may be right and then she loses her son. And if I tell you to drop the matter I shall always think you may have been wrong." I forced myself to accept unpleasantness by voicing the obvious: "Besides, what explanation can I offer her?"

"Blame the police. That's nothing new or strange." I resented his laughter.

"The police meant nothing to her. She believed in you as my friend, and she believed in me."

"I am afraid I cannot advise you, but I shall appreciate a quick decision."

In my perplexity I hated Chand. My mind resisted the finality of decision. After two days I was driven to see her by a sense of guilt. She was sitting on a stool with Chand standing by her. The servants squatted round a circle on the ground cleaned with wet clay. They stood up in confusion on seeing me and I motioned them to sit down. She looked at me and away in silence.

Chand explained: "They are trying to find the thief. They are using rice now. They tried with an old slipper, but it did not turn on any name; nor did the water bowl though I wrote the names myself and put them in. Won't you stay and watch?"

Curiosity offered distraction and I stayed.

One of the women said, "I asked the Fakir Sahib last Thursday of the New Moon, and he said it is not lost but is in the house."

Chand said angrily, "If that were true it would have been found by now." One of the men interrupted:

"Say a prayer over a knife and put it in the

Holy Book, and the thief's guts will be cut to shreds. He will bleed to death, I tell you."

She said drily, "If he loses his life will it give me what I have lost?"

"But our names will be cleared," the man replied aggressively, and the others nodded.

"Who darkens your names? I blame only my fate." At the rising note of hysteria in her voice I moved towards her, but Chand was already calming her.

A woman in clean clothes stepped forward. She weighed rice against the silver coin inscribed with the names of the Four Companions of the Prophet and gave it to each person.

"Shall I take some too?" Chand asked.

"If you, then why not I myself?" she said with passion.

The woman let them chew awhile, then asked them to spit within the circle. Most had swallowed the rice, others spat out chewed paste.

"Look," the woman said. "The rice would have turned to powder and drawn blood from the thief's mouth. There is no thief here." They were loud in their expression of relief, and glad I was a witness of their proven innocence.

"It must have been an outsider."

"How could a stranger know which box to take?"

"Ask the police."

Chand silenced them. "Now we can do nothing but wait for the police."

I said : "I do not believe in this humbug. If my mouth is dry the rice must become powder. Will that make me the thief? Come on, Chand, let us try it for fun."

There was surprised silence. Before Chand could speak she said bitterly : "There is no fun in such matters. What need have you to steal? God has given you enough. And if my son were to steal from me I would that he were dead, and I with him."

"God forbid," a woman exclaimed.

She began to cry softly and Chand put his arm around her in possessive consolation. I felt thrust aside. My decision was made.

A WOMAN AND A CHILD

AFTER five empty weeks of waiting she decided to go to the city. Her husband raised no objection; he never did. He had been hag-ridden by his mother:

"Marry again, my son. Marry again. She has brought us nothing but barren death."

He did not obey, for his wife's passionate conviction that she could and would bear him a child, her tears, her tempers, her accusations, were stronger than his mother's bullying and pleading.

Utterly worn out, he sought refuge in God. Those remnants of his will which he could salvage, he offered to Him. His body submitted to the importunate demands of his wife, but his spirit unwound itself. He accompanied her on her many pilgrimages, but when she cried and implored, "Oh Great One, have mercy on me! Fill my empty life!" he prayed, "Lord, let my life be empty of all but Thee!"

She said, "There is a new lady-doctor at the zenana hospital."

He stopped counting his beads: "There is a Saint's tomb there also."

She answered in impatient anger: "You know I have been there twice already. I have sacrificed goats, I have offered chadars of the finest muslin. What have I left undone?"

"We go to so many places that I get confused. Ah well, I shall make the arrangements."

She had dragged herself from shrine to shrine. "I am a sinner, but, Pirji, if you pray for me Allah will not refuse you."

While she humbled her spirit, she pampered her body. She dressed as a young bride, imagining that from the illusion she would wring the fulfilment of her desire. The bright colours of her 'dupatta' cast kind shadows on her ageing face, and the folds of her clothes hid the hard outlines of her body.

On the train she squeezed her way through struggling, nagging women into the corner nearest the mother who nursed her child. Her eyes slipped mechanically over the others, and returned again and again to the suckling child. The mother drew her veiling 'dupatta' over the child's head; it pulled the thin cloth aside with a dimpled hand, and drew its mouth away from her wet breast. She buttoned her 'kurta', and the smile on her lips was reflected in her eyes. The child pulled at the black cord knotted around its wrist to thwart the evil eye, then slowly reached up to touch the spots of light that shone brightly in the dark eyes looking down.

"Oh light of my eyes," the mother laughed. "Would you blind me?"

She caught the exploring finger between her teeth, and the child gurgled with laughter.

"You are blessed with a beautiful child."

The startled mother looked up at the staring stranger, and, clasping the child more closely in her protecting arms, said, "Allah keep her from the evil eye. My life, my love . . ."

"Masha-alla, may those who wish her evil never prosper! Come, my little one, come to me. See what I will give you."

She held out her hand, and the bells of her bracelet jingled, the glass bangles caught sparkling gleams of light. The child stared curiously with eyes as black as the 'tika' between its brows, then hid its face in the mother's breast. The mother rocked gently, smiling : "My little Rani, why are you afraid? No one will hurt you while I am here." Her eyes shone as she sang softly, "Sleep, my precious one, star of my eyes. . . ."

When the child was asleep the mother asked, "How many children have you?"

"I have none."

"Poor soul! Did you lose them too?"

"I never had any."

"Allah's ways are strange; He seems to have given you wealth, but denied you the richest of all gifts."

The simple kindliness of the woman robbed the

words of their sting. She did not feel resentment, and that was strange. Her own people made her feel unwanted, as if there were a curse on her. They also asked, "You have no children?" but with no sympathy. First they were curious, then contemptuous, and finally resentful of her useless existence.

She remembered one instance particularly. It was her brother's wedding. The women crowded round the scented red bundle that was the bride; custom's licence unfettered their tongues. One of the bride's companions said, "Enough of this! The girl is tired," and she joked, "She must feel the weight within her of her night-old child." Her mother-in-law said scornfully, "How would you know who never felt it?" and someone cut in, "May the evil eye be far from the bride, and may she blossom and flower!"

The mother interrupted her thoughts: "Do not look so unhappy."

"I was thinking . . . why did you say, 'Did you lose them *too*?'"

"Because I lost mine, four of them—all sons. Two died of fever and one was born dead." The mother's voice held no trace of bitterness in its resignation.

"How did the fourth die?"

"Opium. I gave it to him—a little at a time— when I had too much work to do. That was when there was a strike in the printing press where my husband works. I had to take in sewing and embroidery, and the child would disturb me, so I gave him opium. I must have left some lying about, and he took it unknowing, child-like. . . ." The mother, reaching back through memory, stopped, then continued : "It was God's will. He took away what He had given me."

"To some He gives nothing."

"You must not say that. You are not ill, you are not old. My aunt told me about a woman of fifty who had her first baby after carrying it a year or more. Never despair of God's goodness."

"I have prayed; I have been to every shrine. I have tried wearing holy amulets, and drinking holy water. Sometimes I think that all the holy water my husband has drunk has thinned his blood."

"There is a fakir in my village whose amulets have great power. I shall send for one for you. Where shall I find you?"

"I have tried everything; I have even been to hakims and doctors. I am now going to see the lady-doctor who has just come to the City Hospital. You will find me in Nawabganj in the Lane of Attar-makers."

"Fate must have brought us together. I live there too, just above the shop of Ahmad Husain Muhammad Husain, the cloth merchants. I shall bring you the amulet myself. . . . The train is stopping. I hope my husband comes to help me with the luggage. I do not wish to wake the child."

"I can have no such hope. My husband must be counting his beads, busy preparing for his arrival in heaven. I suppose I'll have to go and look for him. It is he who ought to wear the 'burqa'. . . ."

She wasted little time in getting to the hospital.

The doctor croaked like a bird of ill-omen. "You cannot have a child. I can operate, if you wish, but I promise nothing. . . ."

In panic of the knife she thought of the promised amulet, and sought out the woman she had met on the train. Until it was brought to her she existed in a suffocating darkness vibrant with doubts and fears. She wore it, and drank the holy water in which it was washed. The weeks of waiting that followed were as empty as her womb.

She returned to the hospital.

During clinical examinations her body had accepted the tearing of veils of prudery; now it was ready to accept a tearing of its very tissues unto the death that concealed itself within her and made barren the seed of life. For ten days she lay in the hospital, and was surrounded by the sounds of motherhood. She could hear the cries of women in labour, and was bitterly envious of their fruitful agony. She could hear the sounds of babies crying in hunger, and her dry breasts ached. She could hear them cry fretfully, and her empty arms longed to hold and soothe them. Then in bitterness and despair she wished them dead, all the sounds of life hushed, all fertility struck arid.

During visiting hours she picked out the rapid, eager footsteps of children in the passage. Sometimes curious ones peeped into the room, then scampered off. Not one of them came in.

Two days before she was to leave her friend came to see her, but without the child.

"Forgive me, sister, I could not come to see you for the little one was ill, and you know how frightened that makes me."

"Where have you left her now?"

"She is with the doctor. You told me that the lady-doctor was clever, so I brought her here. I'll bring her to see you when they have finished examining her."

"You must take great care of her; she is very precious."

"How well I know it! I know that I can have no more children. I wished for a son, but God has willed it otherwise. Now you will have a son, and I shall share your happiness."

The day she was leaving hospital the sweeper-woman came to her for the old clothes she took as her due. She threw them on the floor, careful not to touch this hag made impure by the filth and excrement she was ordained by birth to clean. She hated the woman, her ugliness, her pitying references to the operation. She disliked the secretive manner with which she came near and whispered, "I can tell you something of interest to you."

"What do you mean? I want nothing from you."

"So many come here like you hoping to have children. So few have them. I can help you if the doctor cannot."

"I do not want your help."

"You never can tell. If you ever need me, you can send for me."

She put on her 'burqa' and followed her waiting husband to the curtained tonga.

The familiar empty pattern of waiting days and weeks followed. In the midst of his prayers and meditations her husband grew restless.

"Soon the pilgrims will start for Mecca. . . ."

"You and your pilgrimage! God knows you'll never be too old for that."

The bond of life's expectancy that held them together grew strained. She became increasingly conscious of her dislike and contempt for this weak, meek man. Her affections shrank and drew themselves into a focus of intensity. All the love that she stored for her unborn, she lavished on the child she had seen on the train. It became the only reason for continued existence while she waited for life to begin within her. She dressed the little one like a doll. She delighted in the child's pleasure in each new gift. She prepared special food and sweets for her. The waiting days lost their blankness.

The simple mother was drawn to her by the common bond of their love, glad the child was given all those things which she herself could not afford but longed to give. One day the mother laughed and said, "She is more your child than mine. She will not rest when she is away from you."

"She will never be away from me. Will you, my love?"

The child ran on unsteady feet, clung to her and called her "Amma!"

From that day a sense of possession grew in her. She became jealous of the mother, grudged her the time the child was alone with her. Her fevered imagination made herself the mother.

Two months after her return from the hospital she sent for the sweeper-woman.

"You said you could help me. What can you do for me?"

"If you eat the cord of a first-born baby you will have a child. I can get it for you from the hospital as I have done for others."

"Get out of my sight, you ill-fated witch!" She shuddered with horror and loathing.

The day came when in desperation and anguish she sent for the hated woman again. It was not long before the woman returned with a bottle wrapped in a dirty newspaper, took a rupee in payment, gave gratuitous advice, and went away triumphant.

The day that followed was one of exhaustion. Each time she retched she felt as if the death within her would be forced out of her womb, take the shape of a monstrous jinn and possess her completely.

When the child came to see her, after what seemed an unlimited stretch of time, she was still in bed. She stroked its hair with trembling hands, and her caressing voice was weak. The child played for a while near her, then, disappointed when no new toy was given, no new games played, went home. The mother came in the evening.

"What is wrong? I understood from the child's chatter that something had happened to you, and I came as soon as I could get away from my work."

"Nothing is seriously wrong; my stomach is upset."

"It must be this horrible food one gets now. It would not surprise me if these wretched butchers fed us on dog's meat or human flesh."

"How can you talk like that? Give me that bowl; I feel sick."

"Poor, poor thing! Why don't you send for a hakim?"

"I hate them; I hate all of them."

Surprised by the venomous bitterness in her voice the mother said, "Please don't be angry. I merely suggested it because you look so ill."

Again for some time the child stayed away and the house was unbearably silent. Her longing for the child's presence became an obsession. At last she sent a desperate message, and the mother brought the child that very evening. She thought the mother an alien presence.

"My little darling, why did you stay away from me?"

She strained the child to her until it gasped for breath and struggled away from her arms.

"I was busy," explained the mother, "and she would not come without me. I think she was frightened that day when you were ill."

"Frightened of me? Nonsense!" Then she added suspiciously, "What kept you so busy?"

"I have a lot of preparations to make before I go away to the wedding. . . ."

"Wedding? What wedding? You are keeping secrets from me. You are hiding what is really in your mind. You want to take her away from me because you are jealous of me."

The mother was bewildered: "What do you mean? Why should I be jealous of you? I've always been grateful for the love and happiness you have given my child. I had not expected the marriage to take place so soon, and was quite unprepared. That is why I had so many things to do all at once."

"Whose wedding is it?"

"My brother-in-law's. I shall be gone only a month or two. . . ."

"A month or two! Leave the child with me, please. You know I will look after her well enough. Will you stay with me, my little one?"

The mother laughed and added, "Or will you stay with me?"

The child ran to its mother and put its arms round her neck.

"Come to me, my love. I will give you sweets and toys and pretty clothes."

The child ran to the other merrily. The mother teased, "You greedy little pretender!"

That night she felt the house a shell. It held no laughter, no prattle, no unsteadily swift footsteps. Emptiness was around her and within her. If she screamed her voice would be lost in it and no one would hear her. Just as God did not hear; the Saints did not hear. If she was to live in silence why should others not share it with her? Why should another have what was hers by all the rights of desire and longing and sacrifice? Would it be easy to say "God's will be done" when His will left no hope?

Her head was heavy and throbbed with pain. She knocked it against the wall again and again. She felt the softness of cloth against her aching forehead, and through tear-blinded eyes she saw her husband's 'kurta' hanging on the wall. A flame of fury and hate burned through her. She sprang

145

up and wrenched the flimsy muslin garment off the peg and tore it in shreds. Her impatient teeth bit and strained at each resisting seam. The frenzy burned in a focus of sizzling green.

The next day the child came without its mother. She dressed her in new clothes that shone like shoots of grass rain-washed. "My pretty one, your mother could not give you these." She gave her a doll that opened and shut its eyes and said *ma-ma* and made the child clap its hands and laugh. "Your mother cannot give you this. What can she give you? Not even love—not love like mine. You are mine, my precious one, my own!"

The child stopped laughing, clutched its doll and puckered up its face with fear of the tear-splashed twisted face so near. It tried to run away and cried out, "Amma! Amma!"

"I am your amma. Don't run away from me." She caught the child and crushed it to her breast. It struggled and whimpered, "Amma! Amma!"

"Sh! Sh! Sh! Don't call her. If she hears you she will come and take you away." She pressed her harder against herself to smother its cry, "Amma! Amma! Amma!" The child struggled desperately. . . .

The doll fell to the ground. Its china head cracked against the hard uncovered floor. The child's struggles ceased.

She held the still form tight, and swaying from side to side cried, "You are mine. You are mine!"

GOSSAMER THREAD

H<small>E</small> came back late from the office and went straight to his room. He wanted to shake off the oppressive silence of the streets with their abandoned trams and buses scattered like toys tired children had forgotten to put back in their places. Quiet people walked warily, conscious of armed policemen, and stared at his car with hostility as he drove past them.

His wife heard him come in, told the servant to prepare tea and bring it to the sitting-room, and went there to wait for him. When he came into the room, she felt, with the sensitiveness of timidity, his silence spiked with ill humour.

"You look worried; is anything wrong?" she asked diffidently.

"No, nothing. I'm just tired," and he began reading the evening paper, not wishing to encourage conversation. Every problem that drove branching wedges into his mind was filtered by hers to a simplification that irritated him. If he explained his disquiet, it would become composite of trite sentiments: "Everything is wrong; the world is wrong."

She poured him a cup of tea, and as she sipped

her own her thoughts scattered and danced, resting fleetingly on the children, the servants, the house, herself, then converging on him who was the constant focus.

She said: "I'm afraid dinner will be late. The cook had to walk from the bazaar because the strike started without warning. It's most disturbing."

Her simplification enraged him. There might very well be bloodshed if the strikers decided to defy the ban against the meeting, and all she could think of was that dinner would be late. He thought it easier to pretend he had not heard her.

She attempted another approach.

"Ali phoned."

He looked up with interest. "Did he? When did he get here?"

"This morning. He should ring again any minute."

"Did he say how long he'd be here?"

"Two or three days. I asked him to come here this evening, but he's busy and said he would ring you."

He had turned to the paper again before she could finish the sentence, but his mind had wandered from its menaces down the lifeline between the mentioned name and the secure remembered past.

There had then been no urgent problems but those that were subjective, without external impositions, and with basic physical origins. His ambition—of which he was conscious without admission; and his snobbery—of which he was unconscious—dominated his thoughts and steered his actions. As a student he was extremely popular, possessed all the right attributes, was good at games and successful with women, passed tiresomely necessary examinations with the minimum effort required, and was derisive of those who turned to intellectual and artistic activities because, he maintained, they were eccentric or weaklings. This, he felt, was the general opinion. His material well-being and his generous allowance from home he accepted as unquestioningly as the fact of being alive.

"Have you," he asked his wife suddenly, "any idea where my college albums are kept?"

"Oh yes, of course. Shall I get them out?"

"Not now, but I wish you would keep them handy. I might want to show them to my friends and I cannot ask you each time to search for them."

"I don't need to; but it's so long since you asked for them; they gather dust lying. . . ." but she realised it was useless continuing.

When he had returned home, he found it irksome conforming to restrictions which he had outgrown during his years abroad. It was a release when he joined a firm and was posted to a city modern enough to enable him to live as he wished.

With his charm and his means he soon became a favourite of the smart social set. For some time he was able to preserve himself, physically and mentally, as near an image as possible of the popular undergraduate, cushioned against the jarring impact of external problems by his personal interests. The first shock came when his father died and he had to face financial facts of which he had no previous awareness. Responsibility added new layers to his mind, just as soft living had covered his athletic body with flesh. He changed perceptibly.

"There is an invitation," she said, "to the reception next week. Shall I accept it?"

"God! they are a bore." He did not look up from the paper.

"I'll refuse it then."

He felt irritated by her literal mind and said sharply: "We might as well go. There is no point in offending people."

As a concession to his mother's importunity, and seeking refuge in professed cynicism, he had consented to marry the simple, immature girl she had chosen for him. She was decorative enough and submissive enough to increase his self-confidence. But from under the strong seal of his personality portions of her own escaped waxlike with visible, uneven edges of which both were conscious. It increased her diffidence and his domination.

"I forgot to tell you, they phoned from the bookshop that the books you ordered should be in by tomorrow's mail."

He looked up with interest. "Did they? I've waited long enough," then added with a persuasive smile: "Will you please go round and get them for me? They are so inefficient, they are sure not to send them for days."

"Of course. I was wondering if the car . . ." but she found herself addressing the newspaper and accepted the relapse into silence.

He was justifiably proud of his collection of progressive—he stressed the word on suitable occasions—literature. His conversion to interests he had once derided as pseudo-intellectual exhibitionism appeared sudden to most of his old friends, but in his mind there had been an unrest for a considerable period of time, and its canalisation in these particular channels seemed natural to him who prided himself on his inherent good sense and judgment. It had started after six years of youthful, thoughtless living.

He had come to an age as uncomfortable as early adolescence. His years had not yet pushed him towards older men, and the younger ones whose company he sought disapproved of him. It was a generation which personified a new spirit of urgent seriousness that found no time for his way of living except to express contempt or worse. He found himself suddenly in a void.

Splintering the brittle silence, she said:

"I wonder where Arun is?"

He looked up frowning: "What made you suddenly think of him?"

"I was thinking of dinner, and what the cook said, and if there's trouble Arun will be with the strikers and he might get hurt." She said it as simply as a child talking.

"Good God! All you can think of is dinner or a man being hurt. Do you understand what this strike signifies?" He worked himself up to rhetorical frenzy: "The naked struggle of progress and reaction." Then he stopped suddenly, shrugging his shoulders.

She looked at him wide-eyed.

"I know I cannot understand. All the words you use confuse me. I don't understand everything Arun says, but I admire him, he is so good and I hate to think he may be hurt."

There was no response, but she had not expected one and went out of the room to see the cook.

In his search for mental anchorage he found in Arun an assured guide. He provided the link absent hitherto between him and the new generation, being his own age, yet with their outlook. Arun's profound knowledge had given him good guidance, and he spoke with the assurance of one who had learned his lessons well. There was a happy expansion of interests for him; he read a great deal, attended meetings, joined societies, worked on committees. He succeeded in securing a prominent place for himself in this new world; and in the old it was too secure to be lost.

She came back agitated: "The cook says there has been trouble, firing . . ."

"Must you get information from the servants?" He was coldly disapproving.

She stood looking at him with worried eyes. "Isn't it awful if it's true? I was right to worry about Arun."

"You cannot surely believe in kitchen rumours," he said irritably. She sat and stared at him, her brows still wrinkled with worry.

He admired Arun even though he was used as an example by those who said his own manner of living contradicted his professions, pointing out Arun's ascetic self-denial, born as he was to the same standards of wealth and comfort. He coupled his defence with attack by admitting he lacked courage, that he had to think of his wife and children, but that dramatic, individual gestures were of little real value, and what mattered was to think on the right lines and not obstruct progress.

She said sadly: "Now everything will be upset for tomorrow. Do you think we should put it off?"

"Put what off?"

"Our party. Have you forgotten?"

"Oh for heaven's sake, don't worry about unimportant things."

His wife's detachment from the problems to which he attached supreme importance was of little consequence to him. From her he required no mental recognition, but merely an acceptance of those patterns of social behaviour which he put before her. She poured tea as gracefully for a prince as a professor, a ruler as a revolutionary. They lived, entertained and were entertained as always; there had been merely an additional trimming for a new type of guest. Arun had never been able to adjust himself to their way of life, but he himself was convinced that intolerant, puritanical fervour harmed the cause of winning over new supporters. It had sharp thorns that probed too deep. For that reason he preferred Arun's friend, a young mechanic whose convictions were free of all complexes, so integrated that he was at ease anywhere and with anyone. He considered it an attribute of sincerity that they had both reached the same point from opposite directions.

"Will you please," asked his wife, "hurry back from the meeting tomorrow in time for the party?"

"Meeting? Which meeting?"

"I thought . . ."

"Oh that one. I've changed my mind," he said, and getting up, walked out of the room. He did not wish to expose his inquietude. Once again he had to face a mental conflict, this time between convictions and action. It was no longer possible for a man to straddle across two worlds in ideological conflict; the drift apart was swift and a man could not tear himself apart, but must jump to one side.

The telephone rang sharply and she called out: "You had better answer it. It must be Ali."

She heard his first hearty greeting change to a note of nervous hesitation. The conversation was very brief and when he returned she was alarmed by the look in his eyes.

"Who was it? Is anything wrong?"

He did not answer her questions but said quietly: "Will you please see to it that no one comes here? Tell the servants we do not wish to be disturbed."

She nodded in silent bewilderment, and left the room. When she came back, he was walking nervously up to the outside door and back, but she did not ask questions, knowing they would be unwelcome. He seemed to be waiting for the knock which, when it came, gentle and insistent, made him start and hurry to open the door.

She exclaimed in surprise, "Arun."

Arun smiled at her, weary. His thin face was pale and he was breathing rapidly. Her husband shut the door without a word.

Arun said: "I couldn't say much over the phone. I had to know whether you were alone so

I took the risk of going into the restaurant." He added simply: "The police are looking for me."

"The police," she gasped and put her hand to her mouth.

Her husband looked nervously at the door and said: "What can I do to help you?"

"Let me stay here tonight."

"Here?" His voice struck a sharp high note.

"I must stay; I have to stay. It does not matter if they find me tomorrow night, but for one day I must be free. There is so much to be done. Everything depends on it. You've always helped, you must do it now."

"But," he stammered, "they know we are friends, they know me; they may come here to look for you."

"It is because they know you they will not come here," Arun said coldly.

He flushed: "But the servants may see you; there is no place to hide you from them."

Arun pleaded: "It's only for a short while, there must be some place. You don't seem to realise how much depends on it—I came to you because I believed you were the one who would understand best."

He said in agitation: "I'll do anything else you ask. If you need money to help you get away. You must understand too . . ."

He could not continue, frozen by the cold reproachful eyes that looked at him from the ascetic face.

"I understand," Arun said, as he walked slowly towards the door.

She called out softly, "Arun," and as he turned his dead face to her, she said, "Don't go away."

THIS WAS ALL THE HARVEST

―――――――

THE young man's voice pitched a semitone higher when he levered his sagging anxiety with self-assertion.

"I've waited hours. You did give him the note?"

"You saw me take it in; and it's barely half an hour you've been here," said the chaprassi.

Uncertain pique flickered in the young man's deep eyes as he tried to disentangle the rebuke implicit in the words from their wrapping of jocular affability. He said cautiously, explaining without surrendering importance: "I wrote the name of my village in case he did not remember mine, which is common after all, no clue to my personal identity, not like the name of my village, which for all the years, his cares and his responsibilities, surely he cannot forget; for after all, no matter how small it may be, how remote from him now, it did get him where he is."

The chaprassi, confused by the rushing words, was sceptical of their final assertion. "Your village did?"

"Well," said the young man, settling himself on the hard bench, stretching his neck above the frayed edge of his collar, "in a way that small beginnings . . ." he paused, and continued with condescension: "It may sound strange to you, but it is a question of politics. If it were not for that election ten years ago . . ."

The chaprassi cleared his throat, and spat squarely into the heart of the rosebush that grew by the steps of the porch.

"What election?" he asked with bored indifference.

The young man was contemptuous of ignorance. "That election," he continued doggedly, "started his career as a politician." He leaned forward, his hands spread on his knees, broad knuckles straining through the rough skin, his stick-like wrists thrust out of the climbing sleeves of the tight coat.

The chaprassi lifted his turban and scratched the cropped back of his grey head, yawning, his mouth a red cavern between the bush of his beard and trimmed moustache.

"You know," he said, clipping with his words the end of the yawn, "that he is supposed to be here on a private visit, seeing no one, resting?"

"Of course I do, you told me that when I came," the young man answered irritably. "And I told you I am here in this town for a few hours. I stopped here specially. I told you he knows me well, that he said to me, I was always welcome. I told you I have to go back to work, and that is why I cannot wait for formalities." Then his rising voice dropped in disquiet: "As it is I'll be late, and will have trouble explaining. Only death could force them to excuse one from work."

"Death?" said the chaprassi immobilised by interest at the very start of another yawn.

"My sister, my eldest sister." The young man shrugged his narrow shoulders, refusing to add to his present anxieties the dark weight of vain sorrow.

He mused: "Curious thought! Had she not died, I would not have been able to come here to see him. And it was she who proved my sincerity to him ten years ago."

The chaprassi was shocked, and being now doubtful of the young man's sanity did not interrupt.

"Was it the day before the polling or the day itself? Oh the tension! the excitement! And suddenly that message, from my mother sending for me, saying my sister was ill, maybe dying. How could I go? I sent money which I borrowed, asking her to send for the best hakim or doctor."

The chaprassi interrupted in horror: "You did not go? Though she may have died? It was your duty . . ."

"My duty?" cut in the young man angrily. "To whom? The living or the dead? The past or the future? To my family or my faith?"

The chaprassi stared in uncomprehending,

censuring reproach and the young man was shamed involuntarily, and continued in self-justi- fication : "My mother had so often before thought her dying. Besides, the hakim I sent saved her."

"No one," corrected the chaprassi, "can save another from death. That is an appointment that must be kept, even he," jerking his head towards the inside rooms, "can't say he's too busy for it."

The young man felt annoyed, resentment was his personal privilege.

"He must be busy not to have sent for me yet. At least I am able to wait here. In the old days I could not even peep over the top of that hedge." He waved his arm to sweep into its circle the green and gold of the garden. "Even if I'd crept somehow as far as this porch I could not have paid my way in."

The chaprassi said angrily: "What do you mean? If the gentlemen gave us anything it was not because they were forced . . ."

"Weren't they?" the young man said sarcas- tically. "Gentlemen! Fine gentlemen in fine clothes who let their wealth, their pride, their birth be trampled by the authority of the officials before whom they crawled. But it's different now." He was buoyed by his contempt for the chaprassi whom the old order had corrupted. He felt a per- verse pride in each frayed edge, worn patch, darkening spot on his clothes as underlining his personal integral worth which gave him the right to come to this house expecting a cordial welcome. He wished to thrust his shabbiness at the chaprassi and say, "Look, I am here in spite of this. . . ." He checked his thoughts, "Not 'in spite of', there being no shame in poverty," and excused himself that he had thought from the point of view of the ignorant chaprassi.

"Yes," he nodded his head with satisfaction, "it's different now."

The chaprassi said sceptically, "Maybe," then with reminiscent regret: "The sahib and memsahib were kind to me."

"Kind to you? That was enough that they should have been kind to you. What did it matter what happened to others, to the country? Sold into slavery with kindness!"

The chaprassi stared with distaste at the declaiming young man, and said irritably:

"Your fine words don't fill my stomach any better than before, if as much."

The young man stared at the chaprassi's ample girth.

"Mine was never so well filled as yours; and my back and my head felt the blows of your sahib's police, softened by no kindness."

They glared at each other, and the chaprassi spat again, missing a yellow rose, while the young man pulled his collar away from his neck with clawing, trembling fingers.

The silence between them was filled with the

sound of the wind through complaisant leaves, and the noises of the indifferent busy road beyond the hedge. The young man felt the weight of expectancy press upon him and looked under lowered lids at the chaprassi who was his only link with the closed house.

He coughed, stood up, stretched, walked to the steps of the porch and back to the bench, then said placatingly, "Why do we quarrel, brother, over what is dead?" The chaprassi's old eyes held suspicion momentarily. The young man felt in his pocket, drew out a flat tin box which he opened and held out:

"Have some cloves and betel nut."

The chaprassi responded to the conciliatory gesture readily because he had been surprised into unpleasantness; and he was glad the boredom of afternoon duty could be relieved by friendly conversation.

"I am a simple man . . ." he began.

"You are fortunate indeed," said the young man. "That is what we need in the world, simplicity and brotherhood. What else could bring me here, a poor schoolmaster in a municipal school?"

The chaprassi nodded his head, still not quite understanding this peculiar young man. Then, because he wished to talk of things within reach of his mind, he said, "You said something about your village and him being here?"

"Is he?" said the young man with heavy humour.

"I gave the paper you gave me to the secretary sahib," the chaprassi said to extenuate himself of responsibility. "They must be working still."

"I must go very soon. Perhaps you could see if . . ."

"Oh no," exclaimed the chaprassi hurriedly. "Oh no, I couldn't. I'm not supposed to."

"Ah well!" sighed the young man, "I'll wait as long as I can," and he sat on the bench again, resting his head on the wall.

"Maybe you could tell me about the village and the election?"

"The election? Oh yes, that election." Interest revived him. "That was an election! What days they were! He must remember them too. We walked from village to village on roads no car could use, dust choking our throats already dry with arguing, persuading, explaining. We, the young ones, the students, sorry for the elders when we had time to think of anything but our work. Nights of sleeping anywhere we could lie down, in rest houses, in huts, on floors, on bug-ridden cots, after endless days. There was little time to waste on eating, and we carried baked grain in our pockets, eating it with 'gur' when we had it. . . ."

"Like labourers," laughed the chaprassi.

"Yes," nodded the young man, "we were labourers, building a new world."

The chaprassi again groped for understanding, and not finding it spat at the yellow rose.

"When we used the car on roads that were holes put together with broken stones or dust, it would sometimes be more trouble than a bullock cart, boiling over till it seemed about to burst or burn. We pushed it for more miles than it carried us, I think."

"Was he with you?" asked the chaprassi.

"Most of the time except when he had to go for important meetings."

"Imagine him pushing a car and eating grain," laughed the chaprassi.

"And why not?" said the young man with returning impatience. "Are not all men equal?"

"Well, well," stammered the chaprassi in surprise. "I do not think so; it doesn't seem so to me."

"You think only of appearance but . . ." began the young man.

"Go on with your story, brother, a simple man like me can't understand your clever arguments."

"Where was I?" said the pacified young man.

"Tell me about your village."

"Ah yes, my village. Had my father been alive it would have been simpler; he was well thought of, greatly respected. My mother she could think of nothing but complaining: 'What will happen to you? What of your college? Leave such things to rich men, you have to earn your living, what do these elections mean to poor people like us?' Women understand nothing of these matters."

"Elections!" interrupted the chaprassi. "My brother was of the same opinion as your mother. 'These fine fellows,' he used to say, 'they come when they need your help to beg you a favour, or buy it if need be, then they forget you're alive.'"

"That may be," said the young man, "but this election was different." He seemed lost in a dream. "It was not for one's self one fought, not for jobs nor position, but for one's faith, with a burning fever."

The chaprassi looked reproachful: "I thought you said there was an interesting story to tell."

The young man drew a deep breath, and pressed his fingers over his eyes: "Ah yes, I was forgetting, but how long do you think he will be?" and the despairing impatience of his eyes struggled to force open the closed door.

"Not longer than your story, maybe," smiled the chaprassi, waving a fly from his face.

The young man suppressed a sarcastic retort, remembering the necessity of the chaprassi's good-will.

"Yes, my story is a long one. Elections, you may know perhaps, are not simple."

"Not straightforward," interrupted the chaprassi, anxious to display his knowledge. "I've heard tales from my brother. He told me what happened during the election in his district. The Raja Sahib was not certain about some of the men who had promised their votes, and as they controlled many others too it was a great worry to know how to make sure of them.

"My brother says just before the election the Raja found out they were definitely going against him, after taking his money, mind you. . . ."

"There is a way of stopping that, I know," boasted the young man. "It's like this. You say to the man, I'll pay you but you must bring your voting paper back, don't put anything into the box, just pretend. Then a safe and trusted man is given all the papers and puts them in with his own. I learned everything in that election. One must, to win, strike at the opponent's weakest point, no matter how."

"My brother," persisted the chaprassi, not to be outdone, "said the Raja thought of a good way out too."

"How did your brother know?"

The chaprassi said, "He was one of the men to whom it happened."

"What happened?"

"If you stop interrupting, I may be able to tell you."

"I thought you wanted me to tell you my story."

The chaprassi ignored the young man's sour words: "On the day of the election he fed them well, such food as they'd seldom seen . . ."

"I know, I know, pulao, zarda, roast spiced fowl, silver-covered betel leaves, sherbet . . ." his hunger dwelt on taste and smell, but the chaprassi continued undeterred.

"Then a bus came to take them to the polling station. They thought the driver was taking a short-cut to it, but after an hour they began to wonder, and then the bus stopped and nothing could start it. The driver worked like a bullock at a waterwheel over it, but there it was; they did not know quite where except that it was nowhere near the place they had to get to. Besides, who could walk in that heat, after that meal? So they waited inside the bus, and what was the use of cursing? They slept until the bus was repaired. By then it was too late to do anything but go home. My brother said it was obvious. . . ."

"What happened to us was different," said the young man, "but maybe you don't want to hear it. Besides I must go very soon."

"Wait a bit longer, brother. Never lose patience when the end is in sight. Your story will make time pass quickly."

"Well, it was as your brother said, some men's votes are more important than a hundred others. It was so with the headman of my village. He was respected and feared not in that village alone but in all that district. All we needed was his goodwill. There we were for two days and two nights, talking and arguing, talking and arguing; and it was like dropping stones into so deep a well you could walk yards away and come back before you heard the splash. If only he would give his word, the district was ours; but no, he was like a washerman's donkey that would not turn from the river homewards. Not even *he* could persuade him. Have you heard him speak?"

"Not more than a few words," said the chaprassi. "I have no work with him."

"I didn't mean that," said the young man impatiently. "It's when he makes a speech; his words would make the milk flow from the dried breasts of a bereaved mother."

"And yet," said the simple chaprassi, "that headman was not moved?"

"Because his eyes and ears were stopped. I suspected something the moment I spoke to him; I knew he was affected by me because he was shamed and angry. I knew that I was the only one who could make him change. I reminded him of my father and of the salt they ate together, their friendship that made them more than brothers, and me more than his son because I was fatherless and came to him for the help my father would have given. How could he turn me away and shame the dead, break faith with them for the sake of strangers? You should have seen the tears in my eyes, how real they were!" The young man laughed proudly.

"He must have been bribed," said the chaprassi, triumphant at his sagacity.

"He was too good a man to be tempted by money," explained the young man, "but every man has his weakness, and what does a peasant love above all else? You know and I know. Specially if he has owned it for generations. . . ."

"His land," said the chaprassi simply.

"Exactly," nodded the young man, "and suppose he can add to it, is it not a temptation? There are ways and means of finding things out. Though we knew the Government Officials were using their influence against us, it was from one of them we learned the secret. You see he . . ." and the young man looked towards the door, "was related to the police superintendent, who told him the story when he thought it was too late to do anything about it, and I was told so that I could somehow use my personal influence, but how could I? One cannot accuse a man one addresses as a father."

"What was it?" asked the curious chaprassi. "You have not told me."

"Well, it was briefly that if he voted against us the 'patwari' would make some changes in the land records whereby the boundaries of his land would be considerably extended."

"No, that is not possible," objected the chaprassi.

"Everything is possible if one has the power to do it," said the young man sharply. "Besides, if you don't believe me . . ."

"No, no, brother, what happened then?"

"We said to him, 'You are an honourable and good man, and your word is above all price, therefore you must have good reason to withhold your help from your brothers in the service of their faith,' and I made my last appeal in the name of my dead father, but he turned his face away from us; and our words, even as they left our mouths, had no belief in them of success. But at that very moment he struck down our withering hopes there was a wailing in his house, and a distracted messenger ran to him crying that his eldest son, a fine, strong youth of eighteen, was writhing in a fit, bleeding from the nose. It was nothing really, just heatstroke, and one of us, a medical student, looked after the boy; but to the boy's father it was a sign from heaven, a punishment for betraying those with whom he had broken bread and eaten salt, and for his sinful greed. So that is how we won that district."

"That was Fate," said the chaprassi.

"Fate?" said the young man. "Maybe, but one can't just sit and wait for Fate, one must fight."

"I hate fighting," said the old chaprassi.

"Did you ever," said the young man militantly, "know of a baby born without pain and blood?"

"I hate blood," said the shocked chaprassi.

"But you like being a father? When a new world is born one is its father and mother."

"What new world?" asked the chaprassi, but before the young man could answer there was a sound of approaching voices and footsteps near the door. The chaprassi sprang to his feet, pulling his long coat, straightening his turban. "That must be the secretary sahib," he hissed in warning.

The young man got up slowly, the fingers of one hand straining at his collar, the other tight-fisted.

The secretary walked forward with an air of bustling authority.

"Chaprassi," he called out, "order the car and quickly."

"This very moment, Sahib," said the chaprassi, himself again, obedient and efficient.

The secretary's uninterested, questing eyes brushed the frayed figure of the young man who had moved forward.

"I sent in my name," he said diffidently. "Half an hour ago," he added, not complaining, but explaining his presence.

"Oh yes, yes, of course. We have been busy, very busy. Is there anything special you wanted?"

"Oh nothing . . . I wanted nothing. . . . I was passing through . . . I had no other time. . . ."

"Well," said the secretary, "I'm sorry, but we

have been busy," and he hurried back into the house.

The young man stared after him silent, puzzled. The chaprassi came back, and stood alert, keeping his eyes on the door.

"Who did you say that was?" said the young man, troubled and frowning intently.

"The secretary sahib."

"Where have I seen him? Where could I have seen him?"

"About twelve years ago, he was a deputy in this town. I worked for him then."

"Twelve years ago? Ah." The breath left him in a sharp sigh as the young man muttered: "Of course I remember him; he was the one who tried us after that procession the police charged."

"Shh," cautioned the chaprassi as the door opened again.

The brooding eyes of the young man cleared with the light of joyful recognition. He saw the now greying hair, the lines of the familiar face, the greater stoop of the shoulders, as tributes the years had paid to this man's burdening responsibilities. He was carried forward by his enthusiasm, and his greeting was a homage. Then in sudden arrested movement he felt the halting touch of the unrecognising look, the unaware politeness of his greeting's acknowledgment.

The chaprassi was standing by the car in trained humility.

"This, Sir," explained the secretary, "is the young man about whom I just told you."

"Ah yes," the sound of the well-known voice revived movement in the young man, and his mouth quivered in a nervous smile as he prepared his reply. He heard his name and the name of his village repeated once, twice, as if they were probes piercing thickened crusts overlaying memory; then the questioning voice said in distant politeness: "Yes, yes the name is familiar, very familiar. I think I've seen you somewhere. . . ."

The young man did not care to remember what followed, was said or not said. He moved back until the edge of the bench pressed against his legs, and stood there motionless till the car was out of sight.

WHITE LEOPARD

HE seemed to me a curious character; and because I expected from him automatic obedience as from the other servants, my first agitated request became an angry command.

His look had now a tinge of pitying contempt, and, ignoring my consequent anger, he turned and began to walk slowly away. His broad, bent shoulders drooped and the weight of the great frame of his body, above which his shaved head with its religious tuft of grey hair seemed disproportionately small, bowed his legs and gave to his walk a rolling movement on his large splayed feet.

"Didn't you hear me?" I raised my voice. He stopped and looked at me with accusing small eyes, pushed in by protruding cheek-bones.

"I did," he said sadly.

"Well, well then!" I found it hard to speak.

"I thought," his voice was deep with regret, "I thought a daughter of this house would grow up carrying a sword in her hand. Instead," he sighed, "you are frightened of a lizard."

"Oh," the breath drew out of my defeated lips, "Oh." I was a child caught cheating.

He was the watchman in the house, but one

175

could not circumscribe him within any such classification; he was so much else that escaped its bounds. He was always the one to turn to in an emergency, whether it was a pipe that leaked, a lock that had to be broken, a cheque to be cashed, a coat of paint needed on a door, a prescription made up at the chemist's, a pane of glass repaired, or the house whitewashed. He could get everything done quickly. The servants and workmen obeyed him more than those who paid them.

He was arbiter in their disputes, adviser in their problems. If a naughty child had to be frightened into obedience it was with threats of being punished by him; if it had to be cajoled it was with promises that he would tell it a story. They called him 'Mahraj' and believed he was powerful, wise and holy. Not only did he observe the rituals of his own religion, but in the month of Moharrum he kept a 'tazia' in a specially prepared shed. On the tenth day of the month, the elaborate man-high tomb made of bright-coloured paper and tinsel was carried to its burial in procession. The Muslim servants recited dirges in memory of the martyred family of the Prophet, while he and his sons followed in barefooted, bareheaded respect.

One afternoon as I sat in the verandah he walked by, looking down at his feet whitened by the dust of the drive, absorbed in meditation and not seeing me.

"Shiv Prasad," I called, remembering I had some work to be done.

He looked up. "Salaam," he said, with his wide smile that seemed toothless because his long upper lip hid the small teeth, still firm at his age.

"Salaam." I put off my request seeing how rapidly the smile was gone. "You seem worried?"

"It's that son of mine who adds to my wrinkles. He does not work well, his teacher says."

"Perhaps he doesn't want to learn; perhaps he wants to be like his father."

The smile returned: "That he cannot be; he has too small a heart. But why should I worry? I shall live until my death in this house, and it is for all of you to care for my sons." Then he said more seriously: "You called me not to ask me of my worries. What can I do for you?"

"I want you to take some money to the Bank."

"Certainly," he said, "but have you counted it correctly?"

"This time, yes." I laughed.

"You children, what is the good of all your books and learning? Now here I am, I cannot write my name, but do I make such mistakes? I could count thousands and thousands of rupees and not be half a one out."

"It was a difference of only ten," I defended myself.

"Only ten rupees?" He raised his unruly grey

eyebrows. "Even if it were one rupee"; he stopped and explained: "I did not like the babu saying the money was short. My honour is not cheap." There was no sting in his voice and his eyes twinkled because we were friends.

The mark of the lizard had grown faint!

"How much is it worth? A man's life? One man, or many men?"

"Aha!" he said, eyes reflecting the sly mirth of his smile. "You cannot catch me, if the whole police force of the district couldn't do it once upon a time. I've lost nothing since but my youth and agility."

"But you can tell me. The police and I come to the question from opposite ends. Besides, what difference does it make now?"

"There are some things one can never release from watchfulness. The law," his eyes were wily, "is a bag of tricks. I know the Penal Code by heart, but I still may have overlooked some tiny point."

"Do you know all of it, or only about robbery and murder?"

"I know what I need to know, and that is enough. The rest is a waste of learning." He nodded his head on which white bristles sprouted and which was reduced in appearance by the size of his long ears. "If you learn more than you need, you lose yourself in a jungle and were far better ignorant, because you would not then approach danger, being held back by knowing you know nothing."

"You make me lose my way in all your words. Answer my question."

"Ask your uncle. What he knows is all that can be known." Then to escape me he smiled. "When I was young and my work made it necessary, I could hide among the rafters like a lizard."

There was never a satisfactory answer and always an element of fantasy in what was said of his early life. Events were so far pushed back in the minds of the two old men, Shiv Prasad and my uncle, that revived memories were like scenes from a broken film, put together in wrong sequences and run through a damaged machine that could not regulate its speed, blurred images, raced through some, and stopped at irrelevant points.

My own mind reconstructed it as a projection of shadows, because one's arrogant youth denied the reality of youth and daring to two men, cautiously wise and conventionally old.

Their first encounter was clear in their minds, but who actually betrayed Shiv Prasad neither remembered, except that it was shortly after the repetition of the gang's robbery with violence had incensed the villagers beyond fear. Shiv Prasad had crept back to his village as he sometimes did from the jungles of the foothills where the gang had retreated.

Though no villager would have dreamt of turning police informer, it seemed different to tell my uncle that Shiv Prasad was home. At this point I had to adjust my mind to the fact that my picture of him as a medieval knight of chivalry was no anachronism or fantasy to them, but a piece of the pattern of their lives.

"What chance had I?" said Shiv Prasad. "He had a horse and a gun and I was on foot with just a spear, knowing him as the best hunter and shot in the district."

"If you had not tried to cross that clearing but stayed still I could not have seen you," said my uncle, "and there were no tracks beyond that point."

At the edge of the forest they faced each other. The wiry young man on the horse commanded: "Drop your spear and stand still or I will shoot."

The giant young dacoit answered arrogantly, "I have no fear; that is how I must meet my end sooner or later," but he dropped his spear and stood still.

The young man on the horse taunted the young dacoit for looting his own brothers, despoiling his kinsmen's villages; and the young dacoit said bitterly he had no choice now but to remain with the gang, because he could never get a chance to live honestly.

"What if I give it to you? Will you come with me?"

"The police will get me."

"I give you my word they will not."

"How can I trust you?"

"I have given my word."

"Let me go now, and I will come to your house at sunset."

"And how can I trust you?"

"I have also given my word; and if I come I will prove myself trustworthy."

"If you do not?"

"You may find me again and waste no words."

"If you come, and the police are there?"

"You will be the loser, breaking your word. I lose nothing, but take a chance to gain something. As I live now, sooner or later they will get me."

"So he came to the house," said my uncle, "and stayed ever since."

"But the police?" I asked.

"In those days," my uncle laughed, his age-dimmed eyes bright with recollection, "we were human beings, not mummies in red tape. My friend the superintendent of police agreed to forget Shiv Prasad the dacoit because I believed in Shiv Prasad the man."

"Yes," nodded Shiv Prasad, his tuft of grey hair waving, "it takes as big a heart to trust as to be worthy of trust."

Though Shiv Prasad deflected with smiling evasions curiosity about violence in the dacoit's raids, he related with pride his prowess at planning them, and he drew fine distinctions between his exploits and thieving on a small scale.

"Everyone can't be like I was. Even those sons of mine," he said disparagingly, "would not make good dacoits. They are weak, credulous and with no judgment. They cannot support a job; a job must support them."

Because he was shrewd and knew they were unlike him, and their world not like his had been, he sent his sons to a municipal school, though he maintained: "What they learn will be less than the knowledge in one joint of my little finger, even if they sit on their benches till they get corns."

His mind was free of all curbing complexities, but by no means simple; between him and his object there was nothing but the relative ease or difficulty in removing obstacles that could not be side-stepped.

When he was fifty he saw a woman who pleased him. She came with her husband, both as day labourers, to help the gardener cut the grass grown wild and high during the months of the monsoon. Crouched in her dirty faded clothes on the tonsured lawn there was no beauty in her and her age was indeterminate—women like her added the weight of their working lives to their years—but when she walked with a high soft bundle of grass on her head there was a provocative grace in the swing of her hips, in the line of her braced back and neck.

That she was married did not deter Shiv Prasad. He had the husband employed in place of the stableman, who suddenly decided to return to his village.

Shiv Prasad's wife did not object. She had been ill for some years and had a realist's view of her consequent shortcomings; besides, the woman had no status, neither as a wife nor a mother of sons, and could be her handmaiden.

The woman's husband was a meek old man whose bones could not be contained by his flesh-less skin, but crumbled in his hollow-cheeked, cavernous eyes; he dared not object even if he had a mind to do so. Shiv Prasad was not a man to antagonise.

They lived happily for many years until, much to their sorrow, the husband died. The woman did not like the appearance of a widow; and the cows missed their keeper.

In summer, coming home late at night I used to see them when the husband was still alive: six in a row sleeping outside the porch on mats spread on the drive; and in winter, wrapped cocoons in quilts inside the verandah which gave an illusion of warmth.

I used to wonder at the effectiveness of Shiv Prasad as a watchman. He scorned the usual prac-tice of walking at irregular intervals round the house coughing and uttering weird noises to sound alertness. The house stood within deep encircling grounds and it would not have taken much skill for a thief to break in while Shiv Prasad slept in the midst of his assorted family.

When I questioned him once, Shiv Prasad was amused, and I was conscious of my naïveté that expected from him anything prosaic and common-place. His system was very simple, very logical and traditional. He demonstrated it specially when there was need for extra precautions on the occasion of a marriage with many guests, money, jewellery and valuable presents collected in the house.

"Who do you think I get to help me? Police-men? Ah no, but men the police live by." His eyes gleamed. "It's easy to understand. I know all the —well, let's call them thieves. If I don't know them personally, I know of them. Firstly, they would not rob this house which is my house, this family which is my family. Secondly, it would not be in their interests to go against me."

He sat on the steps and pulled his 'dhoti' care-fully over his knees while a sly drollery mingled with affection in his eyes.

"Why?" I persisted.

"There are reasons," he laughed.

"I've seen strange people pass by, and heard they go to see you. Who are they? Why do they come to see you?" I hoped his answers would hold some revealing clues.

"I'm an old man; I've lived through many

experiences. I can help the sick in body with my knowledge of old medicinal herbs, and the sick in spirit with charms and prayers."

"And people in other kinds of trouble?"

"Maybe," he smiled, "maybe."

He stood up on his bent legs, dusted his shirt, straightened his back that drooped again and said sadly:

"Nowadays men break the law without honour and with meanness, not because of injustice; even the rich do it to get richer. One must live with self-respect; that is what I want from my sons. But," he mused ruefully, "they are chicken-hearted. It is better for them to go to school. Small men should be honest men, or they would be mean criminals."

Though he tried to hide it, his life centred on his sons. The elder one, Shambhu, was like a large-boned awkward dog that would come near only because of well-trained obedience when called, and manage a symbolical wag or two of the tail, but welcome freedom to roam. The young one, Rama, fat and slow-moving, was his brother's silent shadow. The father's strong personality had left no mark on them; they were anonymous children.

When Shambhu was fourteen his father thought it time for him to start earning his living. Shiv Prasad had so many contacts it was not long before he came to tell me Shambhu had found work in a near-by office as a peon. Many people preferred to employ young boys as peons to distribute letters and do odd jobs because they were paid less than men, and did as much work. Shambhu had the advantages of knowing how to read and write and ride a bicycle.

I said I was glad to hear the news and hoped Shambhu was paid well.

"Not very much. Ten rupees a month; but it will be increased when he is confirmed after a few months."

Then after a significant pause he said:

"The boy needs new clothes to look respectable."

"Won't he be given a uniform?"

"Not to begin with." Then he said as if I were responsible: "Shambhu's shoes are more holes than leather."

"That is sad."

"It's hard to feed and clothe a family."

"It is."

"You wouldn't like Shambhu to go to work the first day in ragged clothes and torn shoes?"

We understood each other.

"I'll give you as much as I can."

"Why else would I ask you?"

"Did you ask? And why me? The others might give you more."

"Because I know you and I know them. Never waste effort. When you have to make a choice think only of the possible results; if unpleasantness can't be avoided, consider it the price of success."

Shiv Prasad had a Brahmin's contempt for his son's employer. The man had originally been a shoemaker with a dingy shop in the bazaar; but the First World War had transformed Bela Ram into the owner of a large establishment, Bell & Sons. Mr. Bell, a good Methodist, convert, donor of a new wing to the church school, had the office from which he controlled his business and properties on the ground floor of the many-layered, wedding-cake house he had built just off the main street.

As I knew him, Mr. Bell was an obsequious man with a long drooping moustache, white against his dark face. He walked heavily with his feet wide apart because of the fat that wrapped its folds around him and squeezed his breath from his body so that he wheezed constantly. His voice rolled out from buttered depths in a spreading boom, especially when he had occasion to exercise his authority, and that seemed to be often, judging from the noise whenever one passed his office.

Shambhu must have worked satisfactorily enough because he was confirmed in his job, though there were occasional complaints that he had mislaid important letters, not delivered others on time, and lied in explanation.

Shiv Prasad said, "That Bell Sahib, how can he

tell the difference between lies and truth when he lies even about his name and origin?"

Shambhu complained that Bell Sahib (his father interrupted, "Bell Sahib indeed, then call me Mister Shiv Prasad!") was bad-tempered and shouted too much at too little provocation.

His father replied: "Small men cannot fill big positions without letting out the importance that puffs them to bursting."

One morning I was called to the telephone, and the instrument rasped at me at my first "Hullo!" so venomously that I almost dropped it.

"I am Mr. Bell," it shouted in black fury and the sound was of broken glass and tin held together by rusty wire. "Is the Judge Sahib in?"

"I'm afraid not."

"Is anyone in?"

"I am."

"I mean someone in authority. I wish to complain. I have been insulted. I will call the police." The words chased each other in a confusion of bad English and poor Hindustani.

"If you will kindly explain . . ."

"I shall tell the Judge Sahib. I shall ask him to call Shiv Prasad to his presence. I shall . . ."

I could not help ringing off, because Shiv Prasad was at the door and talking, and I had to listen to one or the other, and it had to be Shiv Prasad.

"That is the Sahib Bahadur, I suppose."

"Perhaps you will explain . . ."

"I reminded him of something he has buried under his money and houses, that is all."

"I merely want to know what happened."

"For all that he has changed his name and his clothes he is still a shoemaker, and I am a Brahmin."

"I asked what happened?"

"You and your family can abuse me, spit on me; but that man cannot speak to me or my son as he did. My son sells his service, not his honour."

It took some time to bring his anger to the point. It appeared that the previous evening Shambhu had been sent on some special work, which delayed him, and the office was shut when he returned. He had to take a letter up to Mr. Bell's room, and wait while Mr. Bell read it and drafted an immediate reply. While Shambhu was waiting Mr. Bell left the room for a few minutes, then returned to finish the letter he was writing and asked him to deliver it early next morning.

Shambhu had hardly time to wash his face in the morning when he was summoned by Mr. Bell and accused of stealing two ten-rupee notes from the pocket of the coat Mr. Bell had left hanging on the back of a chair when he had gone out of the room.

Shambhu immediately sent for his father in his distress.

Shiv Prasad said he could not repeat to me all

that he told the great sahib because his ancestry should be of no interest to me. "But I did tell him to be careful. Twenty rupees is a cheap price for a mother's tears, a father's pride and a boy's honour."

"What will happen?" I said stupidly.

"I must find out who did it. Shambhu swears he did not, and few people have lied to me when I wished them to confess."

"You did not hurt him?" I said, apprehensive.

"No," he answered quietly. "If I hurt him I would hurt his sick mother. But whoever it is who took the money I'll find out before the police do or my name is not Shiv Prasad."

"The police? He can't call the police for twenty rupees!"

"He'd call them for twenty pies. To men who get rich as he did money means money, nothing more." Then he said with conviction: "I'm not sure he lost it at all."

"He must have been sure," I protested.

"He's a coward; he cannot admit a mistake, and must shout loudest when he is most ashamed." Shiv Prasad would not cast aside his prejudices. His anxiety must have been less than mine because to my own I added his, imagined by me.

Before the day ended a letter arrived from Mr. Bell saying the money was found in a drawer; he did not know who put it there but implied that Shambhu or Shiv Prasad probably knew better.

When I called Shiv Prasad to tell him about it, his face was impassive. I said:

"I am glad it has been proved Shambhu is no thief."

He looked at me quizzically. "Glad he is not a thief? I feared he might be a mean and stupid one."

RAMU

Ramu lay staring at the stars with visionless eyes. Sleep pricked them with needle-points, and pulled his eyelids down, but his thoughts resisted the heavy weight. He heard the smothered snoring of his father and the heavy breathing of his mother and drew himself up stealthily, resting on his elbows. The mat beneath him rustled, and he held his breath lest any movement should bring the shrouded figures beside him to life. But even the baby was quiet by his mother.

He sat up, and edged off the mat wary of sound, then eased himself up with his hands and walked silently on the soft ground towards the low string bed under the tree. His eyes confirmed his heart's fears. It was empty. He took a hopeless step nearer and his foot pushed the bowl full of water against the wooden leg of the bed. The sound was magnified by his mind and the silence and he stepped back in panic.

His mother, with the quickened senses of a woman with a new baby, opened her eyes, then sat up seeing his dim shape.

"Ramu, is that you?" she whispered in anxious fear.

"Yes, Amma."

"What are you doing here? Is it the dog again?"

"Yes, Amma. It is not there." He wanted to cry.

"What of it? It is only a dog after all. It will come back."

"Woman, be quiet," scolded his wakened father. "Do you want to wake the neighbourhood? Lie down, Ramu."

Ramu lay down with resentful obedience, but he could not sleep, though he breathed loudly and evenly in his pretence. When he was sure his father and mother were asleep, he edged away with the care taught by his first attempt, then stood still a moment before stealthily moving away.

He kept within the protective shadow of the hedge, stepping carefully until he passed the sleeping figures of the other servants, then he walked more easily across the soundless grass of the lawn to the gates of the house.

The road beyond was a wide band of cemented silent emptiness. He forced his anxious eyes to see deep into the distance. There was a sound of movement in the near-by hedge and of the short sharp panting of an animal.

"Moti," he whispered in urgent joy, "Moti, come here. Oh Moti, where have you been?"

The dog stopped a moment, its tongue dripping, wagged its tail wearily, then ran on towards the house.

"Moti—wait for me, come to me, Moti. What is the matter with you?" he called softly.

He followed, sad the dog had not responded, but glad of its return. He was in a hurry to lie down before the silent figures on the ground moved, but he had to reassure himself the dog was curled on its string bed. As he lay he could hear its panting breath, and the sound relaxed his mind and brought him sleep.

In the morning when he woke his father had already gone to his work of sweeping the roads. His mother was feeding the baby, sitting on the ground under the tree. He went first towards the dog. It did not lift its head but looked at him, and very slowly its tail moved in recognition. He caressed its head, saying:

"Moti, what is the matter with you?"

His mother said, "There can't be much wrong if he wanders all night. It is just the heat of the day that affects him. See the hair on his body, like a bear. In this heat even these thin clothes bite us, then how must the dog feel?"

"Poor Moti, is it too hot for you?" he said with affection.

"There is a lot of work to do. You better hurry."

He said, "It is part of my work to look after the dog, isn't it? And Moti is not well."

"These dogs—they are not meant for this country," she went on resentfully. "They are just a nuisance. For the money he paid for it Panditji could have paid another watchman for a year and more to guard his precious house."

"He couldn't have got such a beautiful watch-man," laughed Ramu. "Nor such a good one."

"Three hundred rupees is a lot to pay for beauty, and much good the dog is now. I couldn't sell you for that much, you lazy boy. Stop looking at that dog and think of your work."

"First I must tell Panditji about Moti," he said.

He went into the small room in which they lived and brought out his shirt. It was patched and as dirty as the loincloth pulled well above his bony knees. As he pulled it over his shaved head his ribs strained against their thin dark covering.

He picked up his broom, patted and fondled the listless dog and walked towards the front verandah of the house where his master sat in the mornings, drank tea and read papers.

Ramu stood for some hesitant moments watching him, his bulk weighing down the cane chair in which he sat.

"Salaam, Panditji," he said nervously.

"Panditji . . ."

"Well, what is it?" The deep rumbling voice covered Ramu with confusion and fear.

"It is about Moti," he said nervously.

The newspaper slipped down, and Ramu felt

himself pinned against the pillar by the staring of angry eyes.

"Moti is not well. He will not eat, and he lies quietly all the time," he said quickly to drive away that look with rushed explanation.

"How long has he been like this?"

"Four days," Ramu stuttered.

"Four days! Why did you not tell me sooner?"

"I thought it must be the heat."

"I do not pay you to think." Ramu winced at the impact of the loud anger. "That dog is a valuable dog. I should not have trusted him to a child's care."

Panditji's anger was in proportion to his shame that he had risked so valuable an investment to Ramu, calculating a special servant would have cost at least fifteen rupees a month while Ramu's mother was happy enough her son earned three extra rupees. It had been worth paying 300 rupees for a good watchdog to guard the money and gold he could not disclose by depositing it in a bank. His love of money, and Ramu's love of Moti, converged to a focal point.

Ramu blinked back his tears. "No one could have cared for Moti as I do," he said, not knowing how else to show the love that ached in his heart.

"Do not answer back, little urchin," Panditji roared.

Then he added with a voice toned down by anxiety: "I shall give you a letter to the vet. Take

the dog on a tonga, and be very careful. Come
back in an hour's time."

Ramu brightened and turned to go: "Salaam,
Panditji."

"Ramu, one moment."

He turned back, afraid again, and anxious to
get back to Moti.

"Be careful not to let Moti out of the compound. I have read in the paper a warning that a
mad dog or a mad jackal may be in the neighbourhood. Several dogs have been attacked in the
past few nights."

Ramu felt chilled. "How many nights?" he
asked softly.

"How should I know? Run along now."

"Panditji, how far away did this happen?
Could a dog as big as Moti get there—I mean
could the dog get here from there quickly?"

"Perhaps, perhaps not. It happened near the
Zoo." Panditji was impatient.

Ramu brightened. "That is far away, and it
may be any animal near the Zoo."

"What makes you ask these silly questions?"
Panditji asked suspiciously.

The little boy smiled happily. "It is nothing,
Panditji, nothing. Salaam, Panditji," and he
skipped gaily back, first on one leg, then the
other.

He did his work quickly, helping his mother
sweep the house and the large compound, and do

all the small jobs the other servants found fit only for untouchables. He wanted to be free to stay near Moti and nurse him.

When night came he lay tired by his father and mother. He wondered what the vet would write to Panditji about Moti, and he resented it that no one understood that he should be told first and told quickly. The vet had scolded him as if he had been insolent and presumptuous and wasted his time when he asked questions. Then his heart sank when he remembered what Panditji had said. Where did Moti go at night these last few nights? Why? It could not be Moti who—Oh no, it was too far away. And Moti was not mad. Mad dogs bit people on sight, they ran straight ahead and couldn't turn and couldn't drink water. He turned restlessly. Perhaps he ought to chain Moti —but that would be cruel. Besides, Moti was too weak to go anywhere at all—Ramu was carried by his thoughts into sleep.

In the morning when he woke Moti was not on the bed.

"Amma," he cried wildly to his mother. "Have you seen Moti? Where is Moti?"

"He must be somewhere. Why do you worry?"

Ramu's eyes burned with angry tears.

"You know Moti does not go anywhere without me."

He ran round the house, through the gardens, to the gate: "Moti, Moti, Moti."

Panditji heard the high anxious cry and called loudly:

"Ramu, come here. What is it?"

Ramu shook with a double fear. "It is Moti, Panditji. He has gone."

"Gone!" Panditji roared. "Go and find him or I'll take the hide off you. I told you to be careful. Why did you not chain him?"

Ramu shrank from the menace, his tears flowing saltly into his sobbing mouth, and ran out of the gate.

He roamed the streets for a while where he had been used to taking Moti for a walk, proud when people stopped to look at the great shaggy wolf-like dog beside him. He used to say, "Up, Moti, up," and when the dog dwarfed his thin tiny figure, and licked his face, he felt strong and big and proud that he was not afraid of this fierce-looking animal from whom others sidestepped on the pavement. Now people glanced with unfriendly curiosity at the crying naked child wiping his eyes with his loincloth, and walked on.

He turned back hoping Moti was home, but first he made sure Panditji was not on the verandah. He ran to the bed under the tree. It was still empty. His mother was inside, her eyes red— "Where have you been, you ill-fated wretch? Panditji says he will beat you and turn us out if Moti does not return. He will tell the police it is lost, and then they will come here asking questions. They might take us away to prison. You wretched child," and she swayed crying and moaning.

Ramu crouched in a corner. "Moti will return, he will, he will," he said defiantly, then screwed up his face and cried with his mother.

He hid in fear and did not go out. Towards evening Panditji sent for him, but he told his mother to go instead and say he had not come home. When his mother came back her face had lost most traces of fear.

"Ramu, it is all right. It is not our fault, Panditji says. Moti was mad and was shot last night by the Superintendent Sahib in the Zoo."

"Moti was shot!" Ramu turned his face to the wall and wailed as if beaten with a fine switch. "How dare he! How dare he! Moti was not mad, he was not mad, I tell you."

He kicked his heels against the floor, and clenched his fists in the impotence of his rage and grief.

"Well, if Moti was not, you are. And Panditji said if Moti was mad you will have to have needles poked in your stomach."

"Moti was not mad," Ramu wailed.

He did not work the next day, but lay in the dark room crying. He would not eat. His mother scolded him:

"You will die like a dog too. Get up, child, get up and eat."

She brought him the choicest bits from the left-over scraps that were given them after every meal in the house.

"You know, Amma, they shot Moti, and must have carried him away on a rubbish cart. They didn't care."

"Child, stop crying and eat. You cannot kill yourself for a dog, and you have work to do, dog or no dog," she said impatiently, angry and tired working alone, and nursing the baby. She was sorry enough Moti was dead. Three precious rupees a month were lost with the dog.

Ramu was frightened still of Panditji, but had to go when he was sent for next day. He trembled as he said, "Salaam, Panditji."

Panditji was reading the newspaper: "Ramu, that mad animal is still about, the papers say. Perhaps Moti was not the one."

Ramu was transfigured with joy: "I knew it, I knew Moti was not mad."

He did not stop to say "Salaam" as he ran to tell his mother. Panditji did not notice. He was already speculating whether he could somehow make out a case for payment of damages.

Ramu wanted to proclaim to the world that Moti was innocent. He told all the servants, he ran to tell his friends. By evening his joy had intoxicated him to dare anything for Moti. He found his way to the Superintendent Sahib's bungalow by the Zoo and walked past the gate.

There was a gardener digging up weeds in the lawn. He looked at the small ragged figure. "What do you want?" he asked.

"I want to see the Sahib about Moti." He had courage enough to talk to servants.

"Moti?" the man said suspiciously.

"Yes, Moti—the dog that was shot here." His voice quavered.

"Be off with you. The Sahib has no time for the likes of you," and he chased him out of the gate.

Ramu came back and hid near the gate, his heart aching at the thought that here in this garden his beloved Moti had been murdered. He waited until he saw a car stop near the steps of the house, then turn slowly towards the gate. He stood between the gateposts, and the car stopped with a jerk.

A red-faced man put his head out and shouted: "Get out of the way, urchin."

Ramu called out shrilly, "Sahib, I want to talk to you."

The man was surprised into a moment's silence, then:

"What is it?" he said, intrigued by the strange child.

"Moti was not mad, Sahib."

"What the devil—"

"I looked after Moti, Sahib, and you shot him, but he was not mad."

The man felt a return of his sorrow as he saw

202

the dog lying dead. He would not explain his feelings to this ragged child—why he had to shoot him, what he felt now that there was a doubt in his own mind. His mind found an obvious solution. He took a silver rupee and held it out to Ramu.

"Here, child, if it's money you want."

Ramu stared at the silver coin, then said angrily, "I came to tell you Moti was not mad," and before the car could be started again he was off, a brown shadow running into the dark shadows by the road.

FOR THE BEST IN PAPERBACKS, LOOK FOR THE

In every corner of the world, on every subject under the sun, Penguin represents quality and variety—the very best in publishing today.

For complete information about books available from Penguin—including Pelicans, Puffins, Peregrines, and Penguin Classics—and how to order them, write to us at the appropriate address below. Please note that for copyright reasons the selection of books varies from country to country.

In the United Kingdom: For a complete list of books available from Penguin in the U.K., please write to *Dept E.P., Penguin Books Ltd, Harmondsworth, Middlesex, UB7 0DA.*

In the United States: For a complete list of books available from Penguin in the U.S., please write to *Dept BA, Penguin*, Box 120, Bergenfield, New Jersey 07621-0120.

In Canada: For a complete list of books available from Penguin in Canada, please write to *Penguin Books Ltd, 2801 John Street, Markham, Ontario L3R 1B4.*

In Australia: For a complete list of books available from Penguin in Australia, please write to the *Marketing Department, Penguin Books Ltd, P.O. Box 257, Ringwood, Victoria 3134.*

In New Zealand: For a complete list of books available from Penguin in New Zealand, please write to the *Marketing Department, Penguin Books (NZ) Ltd, Private Bag, Takapuna, Auckland 9.*

In India: For a complete list of books available from Penguin, please write to *Penguin Overseas Ltd, 706 Eros Apartments, 56 Nehru Place, New Delhi, 110019.*

In Holland: For a complete list of books available from Penguin in Holland, please write to *Penguin Books Nederland B.V., Postbus 195, NL-1380AD Weesp, Netherlands.*

In Germany: For a complete list of books available from Penguin, please write to *Penguin Books Ltd, Friedrichstrasse 10-12, D-6000 Frankfurt Main I, Federal Republic of Germany.*

In Spain: For a complete list of books available from Penguin in Spain, please write to *Longman, Penguin España, Calle San Nicolas 15, E-28013 Madrid, Spain.*

In Japan: For a complete list of books available from Penguin in Japan, please write to *Longman Penguin Japan Co Ltd, Yamaguchi Building, 2-12-9 Kanda Jimbocho, Chiyoda-Ku, Tokyo 101, Japan.*

VIRAGO MODERN CLASSICS

The first Virago Modern Classic was published in London in 1978, launching a list dedicated to the celebration of women writers and to the rediscovery and reprinting of their works. While the series is called "Modern Classics" it is not true that these works of fiction are universally and equally considered "great," although that is often the case. Published with new critical and biographical introductions, books appear in the series for different reasons: sometimes for their importance in literary history; sometimes because they illuminate particular aspects of women's lives, both personal and public. They may be classics of comedy or storytelling; their interest can be historical, feminist, political, or literary. In any case, in their variety and richness they promise to confuse forever the question of what women's fiction is about, while at the same time affirming a true female tradition in literature.

Initially, the Virago Modern Classics concentrated on English novels and short stories published in the early decades of the century. As the series has grown, it has broadened to include works of fiction from different centuries and from different countries, cultures, and literary traditions; there are books written by black women, by Protestant, Catholic, Muslim, and Jewish women, by women of almost every English-speaking country, and there are several relevant novels by men.

FOR THE BEST IN PAPERBACKS, LOOK FOR THE

☐ **A STRICKEN FIELD**
Martha Gellhorn

Mary Douglas, a detached American journalist, arrives in Prague in October 1938 and finds the city transformed by fear. Through her friend Rita, a German refugee, Mary becomes irrevocably involved with the plight of the hunted victims of Nazi rule.　　　　*320 pages*　　*ISBN: 0-14-016140-6*　　**$6.95**

☐ **THE RISING TIDE**
M.J. Farrell (Molly Keane)

An absorbing tale of three generations of an Irish family in the first decades of the twentieth century, *The Rising Tide* centers around Garonlea, the huge gothic house which holds each family member in its grasp.
　　　　　　　　　336 pages　　*ISBN: 0-14-016100-7*　　**$7.95**

☐ **DEVOTED LADIES**
M.J. Farrell (Molly Keane)

It is 1933. Jessica and Jane are devoted friends—or are they? Jessica is possessive, has a vicious way with words and a violent nature. Jane is rich and silly and drinks too much. And when Jane goes off to Ireland with George Playfair, the battle begins.　　　　*320 pages*　　*ISBN: 0-14-016101-5*　　**$6.95**